Beyond Safe Boundaries

Margaret Sacks

Puffin Books

ACKNOWLEDGMENTS

my thanks to Tom Russell
and to Rosemary Brosnan

PUFFIN BOOKS
Published by the Penguin Group
Viking Penguin, a division of Penguin Books USA Inc.,
375 Hudson Street, New York, New York 10014, U.S.A.
Penguin Books Ltd, 27 Wrights Lane, London W8 5TZ, England
Penguin Books Australia Ltd, Ringwood, Victoria, Australia
Penguin Books Canada Ltd, 2801 John Street, Markham, Ontario, Canada L3R 1B4
Penguin Books (N.Z.) Ltd, 182–190 Wairau Road, Auckland 10, New Zealand

Penguin Books Ltd, Registered Offices: Harmondsworth, Middlesex, England

First published in the United States of America by E.P. Dutton,
a division of Penguin Books USA Inc, 1989
Published in Puffin Books 1990
1   3   5   7   9   10   8   6   4   2
Copyright © Margaret Sacks, 1989
All rights reserved

LIBRARY OF CONGRESS CATALOGING IN PUBLICATION DATA
Sacks, Margaret.   Beyond safe boundaries / by Margaret Sacks.   p.   cm.
Summary: Elizabeth comes of age in 1960s South Africa as her older
sister joins a secret group opposed to the country's racial policies.
ISBN 0-14-034407-1
[1. Race relations—Fiction.   2. Sisters—Fiction.   3. South
Africa—Race relations—Fiction.]   I. Title.
PZ7.1223Be 1990   [Fic]—dc20   90-32598

Printed in the United States of America
Set in Bembo

*for my mother and in memory of my father
and for
Harold, David, and Wendy*

Yesterday, in the recesses of my wardrobe, in an old, lidless suitcase filled with mementos, I came across my first school notebook, which I had kept over the years for sentimental reasons. It had been carefully covered in brown paper, and in the top right-hand corner, in large print, I had written:

Elizabeth Levin
Sub-A
Queen Victoria Junior School for Girls
Port Me
South Africa
World

The first page was neatly dated *17th January, 1953,* and the *Port Me* on the cover was testament to the fact that at six years old I had been quite convinced that Port Elizabeth, the city we live in, had been named after me.

I stared at those round, meticulous letters touching the

penciled lines at all the correct points of contact until the print became a blur. Over the past nine years, during my rare bouts of spring cleaning, I had avoided discarding the notebook, but this time, without a qualm, I dropped it in the dustbin. I was shedding the past. No longer could I relate to that innocent, self-satisfied six year old. At the age of fifteen I had become a realist. People I loved were dead, and my sister Evie was gone. I knew that so-called friends whispered about her, and the bolder ones solicited tidbits of information, practically begged for confidentialities, which I knew they would then share at their private tea parties.

I tried to recall when my world began to unsettle, when the seeds of change were first sown, and as always, I came up with the same answer: It was that happy-sad day my father arrived home with his bride—my new mother. I was in the standard-four class at Queen Vic, and at eleven years old, wise enough to feel some apprehension, an intuition that nothing would be quite the same again. It was an unfortunate coincidence that the upheaval in our family coincided with the general stirrings of unrest in our country.

1

The rain had stopped and the sun beat down, making everything steamy. The heat came up off the pavement in front of our house where the ants relentlessly tried to drag a dead beetle into a too-narrow crevice. I kept my feet up in the air as I swung slowly back and forth on the wooden gate, careful not to injure the black hordes of ants marching double file as we did at school. Such energy they had in this damp heat! More than the men and women in caps and bright T-shirts playing golf across the road. If I half-closed my eyes and ignored the narrow one-way street in front of our house, the putting green of the ninth hole of the Port Elizabeth Golf Club became an extension of our front garden. I had a whole collection of golf balls to prove what lousy golfers some of the members were.

At last I saw the Salmons' black car crawling over the hill toward our house. Even the ants moved faster than Aunt Rebie drove. She wasn't my real aunt, but Delia, her daughter, was my best friend and had been since the age of six when we both entered that bastion of the British Empire, Queen Victoria Junior School for Girls, which strove, somewhat unsuccessfully, to convert white colonial children into snotty English ladies.

I had told no one at school, other than Delia, that my father was going to remarry. She said she knew—she had heard her mother and father talking about it, but she wished she hadn't known so that I could have been the first to tell her. Although I made her promise not to tell anyone, the word *stepmother* was soon being bandied around at school.

It may have started the day we played Whispers in the playground, a large area of tar-covered concrete where we sat and ate lunch while the burning tar melted stickily into our behinds. Playing Whispers with our hats on was awkward, but the covering did protect us from the sun and from profuse pigeon droppings. Six of us sat in a line and whispered to each other the word chosen by the person at the front of the line. When the last person stood up and gave a garbled rendition of the original word, we would all laugh gleefully.

Sitting next to me that day was Marsha Baum, with her sallow cheeks and perfect ringlets that hung down to her shoulders like shiny, brown sausages. She insisted the curls were natural, but it was rumored that Marsha's mother wrapped her hair in special rags and curlers every night. Even Marsha's sandwiches, made by her doting mother, were circles with layers of color in them—pink anchovy paste and cream cheese—quite exotic compared with my brown bread and jam that Mathilda, our cook, slapped together for me every morning. Perhaps my new mother would know how to make circular sandwiches too, I had thought, watching her take a bite.

When Marsha took her place at the head of the line, I

4

was at the end, waiting eagerly as the word passed from ear to ear. Finally it was my turn to stand up and deliver. I had heard the word perfectly clearly, and although the others had shouted out their words, I just whispered mine—*stepmother*.

"Is it true? Is it true that you're getting a stepmother, Elizabeth?" Marsha had shouted, her ringlets jumping nastily. "Stepmother, stepmother!" My ears were ringing with the word. "I hope she's not a wicked stepmother," someone said, and then giggled.

I had wanted to tell them that I was getting a new mother, not a stepmother, but their faces were shining with malice and I knew they wouldn't listen to me. Delia stood protectively at my side, but I ran off to the toilets—a separate building containing a maze of unlighted cubicles with damp floors. It must have been the foul-smelling disinfectant that had made me bring up my jam sandwich.

Another brightly dressed foursome was on the putting green of the ninth hole by the time Aunt Rebie drove up in front of our house. Delia jumped out, and her mother waved at me and blew a kiss.

"Be good, you two," she yelled through the open window in her deep, husky voice, which my father said was the result of smoking too many cigarettes. I'd once heard my father joke that, in their younger days, Aunt Rebie used to fancy him. She'd take the last appointment for the day at the surgery to have her teeth cleaned (those were the days when she still had her own teeth), and my father would be expected to give her a ride home. If he'd married her, I thought, I'd still have a mother, but then I would be only half me.

5

Delia and I swung on the gate together and watched the putters across the road. Little black caddies, hardly bigger than we were, carried the heavy, leather golf bags.

"What d'ya want to do?" I asked.

"Let's stick out our legs and keep them very still and see who can get the most mosquito bites," Delia suggested.

I had been shooing away the mosquitoes, but now we let the big, black, buzzing bloodsuckers have their fill.

Next door the post box creaked and I saw Fiona Frazer staring at us. She was a fat, freckled ten year old, one year younger than Delia and I, and a convenient playmate when Delia wasn't around. Whenever Fiona wanted to know what was going on at our house, she'd pretend to look in the post box and casually wander over.

"What are you doing?" she asked.

"Getting anemic," Delia replied. I loved the way she knew all those big words. My father said if I read as much as she did, I'd know them, too. But I told him that if I were allowed to go to the "bioscope" as often as she did, my vocabulary would improve, too. "*Cinema,* not *bioscope,*" my father corrected, as he always did when I converted Afrikaans words to English slang. Although I wasn't allowed to see many films, I knew them all because Delia loved to tell a story and she remembered every detail of every one she saw. She also had a picture collection of film stars, including a signed photograph of Elizabeth Taylor.

"I'll join you," Fiona said, sitting on the low, stone wall adjacent to the gate and sticking out her legs. There was no more room on the gate, which was already creaking with our weight.

"There's your dad," I said. Mr. Frazer, in his khaki safari suit, was chipping the ball out of the bunker onto the green. My father was also a golf enthusiast, but he wasn't allowed to be a member of the club across the road for the same reason I'd been refused admission to the Port Elizabeth Municipal Tennis Club when I was nine years old: No Jews allowed.

"Let's see if the mosquitoes like Christian or Jewish blood best," I said to Fiona.

"If I were getting a new daughter," Fiona said prissily, "I wouldn't like her to have red bumps all over her legs."

My feet flopped down onto the pavement, squashing an army of ants. No doubt she was right. I should at least try to look my best when my father arrived from Johannesburg with my new mother later in the day. After all, I had waited for this moment long enough.

Fiona's legs were still up in the air enticing the buzzing insects. "My father says your new mother is Irish, so if she were your real mother you'd be half Christian," said Fiona in her know-it-all voice.

"Don't be dumb," I said, "She's Irish-Jewish, not Irish-Christian."

"You're calling my father dumb?" she said.

"Well, my father is older than yours, and he says she's Irish-Jewish, and he should know."

"If your father is older, he's going to die sooner." And with that prediction, Fiona Frazer jumped off the wall and marched off to her house.

The thought of my father dying and my being left an orphan had always been my one greatest, secret fear, but Fiona Frazer wasn't going to know that.

"Sticks and stones may break my bones, but words will never hurt me," I shrieked at her departing back.

"Your neighbor is so puerile," Delia said, plaiting a

7

piece of hair that fell over her shoulder. "Let's go inside, and I'll give you an Elizabeth Taylor hairstyle that will knock out your new mother."

The house was unusually quiet. Mathilda, the cook, was taking her afternoon rest in her room out in the yard, while Lena, the housemaid and nanny, had the afternoon off, which meant she had gone to visit her family in New Brighton, the African township that my father said must have been named by a cynical Englishman, considering the impoverished housing conditions. My older sister, Evie, was at ballet class. I was very proud of the fact that my sister was a real ballerina and had even refused a scholarship to Sadler's Wells in London, choosing instead to follow an academic career at Witwatersrand University in Johannesburg. As usual, Evie's room was a mess. Clothes and shoes were strewn all over the floor.

"Isn't your sister going to clean up before your dad arrives?" Delia asked. I shrugged, remembering the scene she'd made two years before when my father told us he was going to marry again, and I knew she would do nothing to make our new mother welcome.

"You know, Dele," I said, "two years ago I wanted a mother more than anything, but now I feel kind of scared. What if we don't like each other or what if Evie behaves like a monster?"

"Oh, don't worry," Delia said, pushing me into a chair and draping my bath towel around my shoulders while she snip-snapped the air with the kitchen scissors—the same pair that Mathilda used to clean the Sabbath chickens that still had a showing of feathers.

"Shouldn't we put some newspaper on the floor?" I asked, getting up.

"Yeah, I guess so." Delia was pretty lazy and I knew I'd

8

have to sweep up the mess. I didn't dare ask Mathilda, whose sole territory was the kitchen.

"Look, this is the style I'm going to give you," Delia said, pointing to a glossy picture in *Stage and Cinema,* a magazine she regularly bought at the bioscope. The cover of this issue showed a back view of Marilyn Monroe from head to toe. Her eyes gazed at us over a raised shoulder and her fingers were spread against her legs, which formed a deep, inverted, fishnet-covered V.

Delia could see I wasn't too interested in the pictures. "Look," she said, "Evie is going to university soon, so even if she and your new mother don't get along, it will only be for a short time." Delia pulled my hair forward. "First I'll cut a fringe, then we'll wet it and twist it into bangs." Snip-snip! I closed my eyes as hair flakes dribbled down my nose.

"Anyway," Delia said with a romantic sigh, "your new mother must really love your dad to have waited so long."

"Yeah, that's what I told Evie, and she said, 'Well, Dad is a jolly good catch for someone who's not exactly a spring chicken.' " I put my hands on my hips like Evie did in a bossy mood and swung my head, mimicking her.

"Goll-ee," Delia said, as a chunk of hair hit the newspaper, leaving a few spikes on my arm en route.

"You sound just like your sister. You should be an actress."

I loved it when people said things like that. I knew I could mimic well and didn't need a great deal of prompting to act out whole scenes. "You should have seen the time my father told us he was going to marry again. That was a scene and a half!" I was flushed with the warmth of her praise.

"Tell me! Tell me!" Delia cried, snipping furiously. She

loved our family dramas. Everything was so calm in her own household.

"Can I look in the mirror yet?"

"Not yet, hold your horses just a few more minutes. So-o your father came home from Johannesburg with the big news—gosh, that seems so long ago."

Two years, but the memory was perfectly clear. My father had looked so happy. He had brought us gifts from himself, and from "someone else" who was going to be our mother. And then Evie had flung a damper on all our joy.

"We don't need a mother," she had said. "We had a mother and she's dead, and no one is going to take her place." Her body had stiffened up like a toy soldier's and her face had paled. She took a step toward me as though we were allies. I felt myself shrivel up inside, and I could see from my father's eyes that he was shriveling too.

"I want a mother, I do want a mother," I said, flinging my arms around my father. Evie gave me a poisonous look.

"What did my new mother send?" I asked. I opened the tiny box, and wrapped in tissue paper was a gold charm bracelet with a heart-shaped locket.

"And she said to tell you that for every birthday you'll get a new charm for the bracelet," my father said.

"Her name isn't 'she.' What is it?"

"Lydia," he said, flushing.

"Lydia!" I liked the name and wondered what she would want me to call her.

My father tried to give Evie her gift, but she held her hands together behind her back. "I don't need any bribes," she said, and turned on her heel. We could hear her bedroom door slam shut.

"Why's she so nasty?" I was close to tears.

"She's not nasty, she's just upset. She remembers her mother, but you were just a baby—too young to remember. And don't forget, Evie's been like a mother to you the past few years." He stroked my hair as he said this. It was true. Evie had played mother for a long time. In fact, she had even chosen my name when I was born—Elizabeth, after the princess of England who had been crowned queen the year I turned five.

"Maybe this is not the right time," my father had said in a low rumble, and my heart sank as low as his voice.

Evie had had her way then, but finally, my father announced that he had put off his marriage long enough. Ever since his decision, Evie had been having fits of crying crocodile tears. She would lie on her stomach on the couch and chant, "Everybody hates me," until I would go and tell her I didn't hate her, though the truth was I was beginning to feel that I did.

All afternoon I kept listening for the sound of my father's car and his key in the latch, but by four o'clock when Mathilda came in from her rest, there was still no sign of my father and new mother.

"*Hayi, hayi, hayi!*" Mathilda clapped her hands when she saw Delia and me. "What you do?" she asked, pulling at my chopped-up hair. "You plucked chicken or what! And Miss Evie, she going to be mad hatter with you." Tilly's vocabulary had become more colorful since I had read her excerpts from *Alice in Wonderland*.

Evie probably would be mad. Delia and I had decided to play Big Ladies, and it wasn't difficult to find what we needed among the clothes spilling out of her wardrobe and strewn across the floor. They smelled of stale deodorant and face powder, but this didn't deter us from strapping her bras around our flat chests and fastening her garter belts around our waists to hold up her nylon stockings. Her dresses didn't hide our lumpy chests, which we had built up with the help of cotton socks. Clomping to the mirror in high-heeled shoes, we applied layers of lipstick and rouged our cheeks. Our eyelids were a rainbow of blues and greens, and Delia had even dared to curl her lashes with a repulsive-looking instrument.

"The master he late," Tilly said. "And the new madam, *yo, yo, yo!* She don't like the way Mathilda is cooking, then Mathilda go *hamba wena.*" Her laugh was an expulsion of air through the gaps between her long, yellow teeth and sounded like the water draining out of our bathtub. I copied her, which I knew she found irritating.

"You'll love my new mother, don't worry," I told her.

"No one take place of old madam," she said with a hiss. "She the best. She best cook—she teaching me. She best tennis player, too."

For as long as I could remember, people had been asking me if I was going to be a tennis champion like my late mother. They asked this in the same tone in which they inquired where I had bought my "big, brown eyes." Both questions I understood to be rhetorical, although I must have inherited the tennis gene because I spent most of my spare time banging balls against the side wall of the house, with no care for the dahlias so carefully planted by Cuthbert, the garden boy, who was really not a boy, but a gray-bearded black man. At the end of every hitting session, there would be a row of pink and yellow dahlia heads hanging from fractured stems.

"How you like me to knock your head off?" Cuthbert

often threatened, but Lena found a way to appease him. She would cut off the dahlia heads and have them swimming in bowls on every table in the house.

Delia and I were singing a duet on the dining room table, still dressed in full regalia, when my father and new mother walked in. We hadn't even heard the car crunch up the drive. We yelped, and Mathilda got up quickly from her comfortable position on the couch where she'd been sitting and clapping our performance. She gave a slight bow in my father's direction and held out a scrawny, calloused hand to my new mother.

"*Molwena,* new madam," she said with a giggle before disappearing into the kitchen. Despite her smile, I knew she was making it clear that my father's wife was the newcomer.

Delia disappeared with her maid, who had arrived to walk her home, and I was alone, aware of my clownish makeup and Evie's clothes dragging round my ankles.

"This is the baby," my father said. I was thankful he hadn't noticed my hair. He looked so happy—his blue, slightly protruding eyes were clear as sunshine, and his smiles and laughter made the vein on his large forehead stand out like the river on a map. He hugged me tight, biting down on his tongue and making a humphing noise, pretending to squeeze much harder than he really did.

He was unaware of my discomfort, but my new mother came to my rescue. "You must have had fun dressing up, Liza, but let me help you change now." No one called me Liza, but I liked the sound of it coming from her. Her voice had a soft Irish lilt, so different from our guttural South African English. She took my hand and stroked it and

13

didn't let go as we walked to my room. She wasn't much taller than I was, and far prettier than the photograph I'd seen, which didn't show her shiny, dark curls and smooth English skin.

"When you've changed, I'd like you to show me the house," she said.

The kitchen scissors still lay on my dressing table with some telltale hairs clinging to the blades. "We'll go to the hairdresser and get your hair shaped," she said. "Cutting hair seems easy, but you have to know how."

"What shall I call you?" I almost choked on the question.

"Goodness, I'm sorry, that's the first thing I should have thought about. Lydia, if you like, but I'd much prefer Mom or Ma."

"Or Mum or Mummy, like they do in England," I said in my most exaggerated British accent, and we both laughed.

"So you are a good mimic," my mother said. "Your daddy told me all about you."

My face heated up. She probably knew I had allergy attacks most nights; that I knocked the heads off the dahlias every day; and that after dinner each night, when I walked down the dark passage to my bedroom, I barked like a dog to scare off any burglars who might be lurking there.

"Well, are you dressed and ready to take me on a tour of the house?" my mother asked. This time I took her hand. I showed her the bathroom with my father's shaving cabinet above the sink, and the antique washing machine, which the washerwoman, Emily, used every Monday for the sheets and towels. Everything else was hand washed by Lena. Through the bedroom window I showed her the washing line where the sheets flapped and the towels dried to a crust. I tried to bypass Evie's room, but she pushed open the door. It swung wide to reveal the mess, which was even worse since Delia and I had created havoc with her makeup.

When we reached the kitchen, my mother asked Mathilda to please tidy Evie's room before she came home. I was about to explain that Tilly only looked after the kitchen, but before I could say anything, Tilly gave her awful grin and said, "Sure, sure thing, madam."

I showed my mother the lounge, my least favorite room, with its stodgy, formal furniture and heavy curtains that kept out the sunlight; and my favorite room, the oval-shaped porch, which jutted out from the house and had windows all around with views of the golf course, our neighbors the Johnsons' house, and of our garden with its giant hedge of hibiscus.

Finally, we moved on to my parents' bedroom. My father and Cuthbert had brought in the suitcases and bags and hat boxes. So many hat boxes! I couldn't wait to help my mother unpack—to see her clothes and jewelry and makeup. I flung open the door of her wardrobe, and we both gasped together. Hanging on the rack inside the wardrobe were three tennis dresses belonging to my dead mother—old-fashioned tennis dresses that someone had stored away for seven years and purposely hung back on the rack to welcome my father's new wife.

By the time she returned from ballet class, one bed and one wardrobe from my parents' room had been exchanged with the spare furniture in Evie's room. Mathilda told me she had warned the new madam not to sleep in the dead madam's bed. My mother, who I discovered was equally superstitious, went one step further and exchanged the wardrobe, too. At dinner, Evie was barely civil, and I could hardly wait to leave the table. I went to bed at the first suggestion—something quite unheard of. Evie retired early, too. As I lay in the dark, I could hear her sniffling in her room. I wondered at her unhappiness. Was she repenting? Maybe she wasn't the culprit at all. It could have been Aunt Phoebe, my father's sister, who seemed rather disapproving of the marriage, or even Tilly, who didn't want a new madam. My father had barely spoken at dinner and he looked old and worried. I thought of Fiona Frazer and her prediction about death and age.

"Good night Dad, good night Mom, good night Evie," I yelled at the top of my lungs. At least if anyone died during the night, I would always remember my last words to them.

"Good night, darling." My mother appeared at my bedside. "Don't worry about anything. Everything is going to be all right," she said in her soft Irish lilt.

2

"Red leather yellow leather red leather yellow leather red yeller leather. . . ." The elocution class snickered as someone failed to master the tongue-twister we each had to say at lightning speed. I knew my performance had been one of the best, and so it should have been. I had been practicing for days in the hope of impressing Miss Godwin sufficiently so that she would give me a part in the school play.

"Now gels," Miss Godwin articulated, "let us try Peter Piper picked a peck of pickled peppers . . . and then at the end of class, those who wish to take part in *A Midsummer Night's Dream* should sign up. But remember, rehearsals will be every evening for six weeks and you must be able to attend."

For a moment my spirits sank. My mother didn't drive a car and my father never came home from work before six o'clock. But then I knew my mother would get me there somehow. The idea of performing on the city hall stage enthralled me. Miss Godwin's plays had been staged there annually for as long as I could remember, and every year the costumes and stage sets were more sumptuous. With

Evie's ability to dance, she had always been a favorite of Miss Godwin, and I wished I had her talent.

"Of course, there are not enough speaking roles to include the standard-four class. The ten who are chosen will be the trees in the forest, so you will have to learn to sway and *whoosh!*"

"No speaking parts!" someone snorted in disgust, yet almost everyone signed up, and I knew that with my height I would stand a good chance of being a tree.

"Old chicken legs here even looks like a tree," said Marsha Baum with a smirk, her fat ringlets writhing like live worms in my direction. A few of her cronies laughed. We all knew Marsha would be given a speaking part even if Miss Godwin had to create it herself without Shakespeare's consent. Marsha was Miss Godwin's favorite. She was a born actress and knew how to manipulate the teachers with her dimpled smile and perfect diction. They didn't know about the Marsha who dug holes in her garden and covered them with newspaper so that when her "enemies" were invited to play at her house they would fall in and perhaps break a leg.

The play was all anyone discussed on the homebound school bus. By the time we approached my stop, the subject had been talked out and a hush had descended. I could see my mother waiting at the bus stop and so could Marsha Baum, who now bounded out of her seat.

"Is that your stepmother, Elizabeth?" she asked in a stage whisper, which reverberated to every corner of the bus. Her captive audience of thirty-five girls bounced out of their seats and peered through the windows.

"Are stepmothers really mean?"

"What's it like having a stepmother?"

"Where's your real mother?"

The voices followed me as I jumped off the bus, which had not yet fully stopped. The warm breeze felt cool against my hot cheeks.

"What's upsetting you?" my mother asked, and when I told her she just laughed and said that my friends were ignorant and therefore curious. "We have to tolerate ignorance and spread knowledge," she said. "It's the same with the natives. If they were educated, they wouldn't annoy us by making silly mistakes."

"Like Tilly ruining your best casserole dish on top of the hot stove," I said.

"No. That she did on purpose," my mother said. "There are agitators in the townships who teach the servants these things, and I'm afraid the next time she follows their advice I'm going to ask her to leave."

By the time we reached the house, all thoughts of the play had drained away, and when I thought about it again I decided to keep it a secret from my parents and surprise them when the cast was announced. But I needed to tell someone.

"Evie, can you keep a secret?" I asked. She was sitting on her bed knitting a sweater. *Clickety-clack, clickety-clack,* the needles bounced against each other. She knitted faster than anyone I knew but hated sewing the pieces together, so her garments never looked quite right.

"Who's that for?" I asked.

"For Dad—my parting gift."

"You make it sound like you're never coming back." I laughed anxiously.

"Well, I certainly don't want to come back. What for? I'm not wanted around here any more."

"That's not true. Ma . . . I mean Lydia loves you. She told me and she said that our real mother was a wonderful

19

person and that it must be really hard for us—especially you."

"She knows nothing!" Evie's jaw was beginning to stiffen. "And one of these days you won't be her little darling anymore either. She'll probably have her own baby and you'll just be the stepdaughter around here."

My hands felt clammy. I wished I hadn't walked into Evie's room and couldn't even remember why I had done so.

"So, chump, what's your big secret?" Evie was her old self again, smiling and confidential. These days I had to suffer before she would show friendship.

"I put my name down for Miss Godwin's play. Only ten standard fours get chosen, but I think I have a good chance. I want to be in that play more than anything in the whole world."

"Uh-huh." Evie didn't seem too interested, and I left her mouthing, "Two plain, two perl. . . ."

Lena was drinking tea out of her enamel mug when I walked into the kitchen. She studied my face and said, "Miss Worriedness! You have mother, you have father, you have nice house, nice nanny. You spoilt or what?" I climbed onto her starched lap and was tempted to take a bite out of her thick slab of bread spread with apricot jam, but like any white child, I knew that eating off servants' plates was taboo. Whether this unspoken rule was for hygienic reasons or to prevent white children from depriving the servants of their full ration of food, I never knew.

"Lena, how many children do you have?"

"One boy in Transkei, one boy dead, and one girl adopted who want job here."

"Which one do you love best?"

"I am loving all my children, but the boy he too clever—

20

top of class in the mission school." Her chest puffed out with pride and she beamed. It was obvious to me that she loved her natural child best.

"D'you think my new mother will have a baby?"

"*Yo, yo, yo!* Who putting ideas in this head? Your mother she got enough on her hands right now."

"But Evie said she would."

"Miss Evie know nothing. She very sad gel and making big trouble round here."

"Maybe she'll be happier when she leaves for university," I suggested.

Lena's brow furrowed and the whites of her eyes seemed to grow menacingly yellow. "Bad thing for unhappy gel to leave her house. She can get in big trouble outside. *Yo, yo, yo!*" Lena shook her head sadly. I waited for her to bite her bread, but she was waiting for me to leave.

I went outside with my tennis racket, and by the time I had finished pounding the ball against the wall, my arm felt like rubber and a row of flower heads hung loosely from their stems.

3

I studied the sheet of names for a second time and tried not to let the tears form, because if they did, I knew they would gush and maybe never stop.

"This is not fair," Delia said, hardly daring to look at my stony face. "That fat slob Irmgard Dietrich is a tree, and Marion Bell—ugh! How could she leave you out? Miss G-win is a twit." Delia would not speak the Lord's name in vain even if it was attached to another word.

"Look here," I croaked, "Marsha Baum is Mustardseed. That's a fairy, isn't it? Doesn't that take the cake!" I could barely squeeze the words through the tightness in my throat.

"Well, we all knew Miss Marsha the Shloop wouldn't want to be a tree like the rest of the plebs. And what M.B. wants, M.B. gets." Delia was so mature and knowledge-able. She knew just what judgment to make about unde-serving people.

I was subdued for the rest of the day and Miss Godwin must have sensed my disappointment. At the end of elocu-tion class, she called me aside. "Elizabeth, you were one of my first choices for the play, but when I called your mother, she felt it would be difficult for you to attend rehearsals every evening. And believe me, she wasn't the only one. Many mothers couldn't or wouldn't commit themselves."

My mother! My mother did this to me. I was stunned. The whole week I had imagined coming home on Friday with the news that I was one of the chosen, and my mother was to have smothered me with hugs and kisses in an excitement that matched my own. I smiled weakly at Miss Godwin.

Lena met me at the bus stop and I gave her the silent treatment. "Mouse got your tongue?" she inquired. "The madam she lie down. She not feel too good today. So you can pretend to be happy gel."

Probably pregnant, I thought, just like Evie said, and already she didn't care about me.

When we reached the house, I marched through the kitchen and into my parents' bedroom and threw down my school case. "How could you do this to me?" I shrieked. "You've ruined everything."

My mother raised herself on her elbows. "What are you talking about? Why are you so hysterical?"

Hysterical! How dare she call me hysterical. "You know what you've done. You wouldn't let me be in the school play. Miss Godwin told me. You thought she wouldn't tell me, didn't you?"

"Liza, calm down. This is ridiculous. You never mentioned a word about the school play. I never dreamed it was so important to you. And I'd even forgotten Miss Godwin called."

"I hate you! I hate you!" I ran out of her room to my own and passed Evie in the passage. She smirked as if to say, "I told you so!"

The tears that had been wanting to gush all day now flowed in a steady stream.

"Crybebbe, cry," Cuthbert taunted, staring through my open window. He had been planting seeds in the flower bed under my window and took delight in my misery. I threw a pillow at his grinning face and continued sobbing.

"Your mother, she want you to come and have tea with her." Lena was in the doorway of my room.

"What mother? I don't have a mother."

"*Yo, yo, yo!*" Lena clucked her tongue. "You sad gel, but you bad gel, too. No respect for Mamma, *unyoko* she love you."

"She doesn't love me."

"She don't tell you whole story. I hear when Miss Teacher phone Madam. The madam she say to Miss Evie, 'What you think? You think Liza want to be tree in play?' Miss Evie say Liza don't care about play because trees not talking, only standing in one place all the time."

I entered Evie's room without knocking.

"Now what's your problem?" she mumbled, her lips closed over hairpins as she practiced twirling her hair into a chignon.

"It's all your fault," I said. "You told her the play wasn't important to me." I wanted to scream at her, but I was too worn out from crying.

"Oh, our father's wife trying to turn you against me, is she?" she spat out, looking as though she were about to stab me with the hairpins now clenched in her fingers.

"No, Lena told me all about it."

"The trustworthy servant with oversized ears! You'd take her word before mine, no doubt. Now please remove yourself from my presence."

24

I went and stood forlornly in my mother's darkened room.

"Come here, darling. I'm so sorry," she apologized before I could. "Come get into bed with me."

I climbed into her warm bed, not even waiting to take off my shoes, and clung to her.

"I'll call Miss Godwin and tell her I've changed my mind. But I also have something else to tell you."

"Are you going to have a baby?" I asked bluntly.

"You're my baby," she said, smiling. "Even if I want to I'll never be able to have a baby, because I have to have an operation called a hysterectomy. That's one reason I couldn't have taken you to rehearsals."

"Are they going to put you to sleep?"

"Yes." Her hand squeezed mine. "You'll have to help me to be brave."

"Could you die?" An octopus was grasping my heart and squeezing it so tight that I could hardly breathe.

"No, silly." She smiled unconvincingly and stretched out her hand to reach the bell at her bedside that rang through to the kitchen and servants' rooms.

Lena stood in the doorway. "Yes, madam."

"Where's Mathilda? Liza and I would like some tea now."

"Mathilda, she is out. I will make tea, madam." Lena seemed more obliging than she ever had.

"Mathilda's not playing the game," my mother said sternly, knowing that the message would be relayed in Tilly's direction in due course.

"Madam, my cousin is here from the Transkei and she is looking for cooking job."

"Lena, you call everyone cousin. What exactly is the relationship?" my mother asked.

"She my adopted daughter, child of my dead sister," Lena said.

"Does she have a pass to work here?" my mother asked.

"When Beauty get job, then her madam will get pass for her."

"Lena, you know it's not that simple."

A while later, Lena returned with a tea tray laden with a steaming pot of tea, two china cups, and a plate of scones.

"Beauty make scones," Lena said, and, as if on cue, Beauty appeared.

"Well, you really do live up to your name," my mother said sweetly, and Beauty whispered a thank you. She was very young and pretty with large, soft, round eyes, but she was nervous and twisted her hands shyly. Certainly, Lena would be able to boss her around as she never could Tilly.

This encounter with Beauty made me acutely uncomfortable, as though we were being disloyal to Tilly, who had been part of our family for years.

"My mother's having an operation," I announced to Lena and Beauty.

"*Hayi!*" Lena's mouth opened in surprise and she touched her cheek.

"A hysterectomy," my mother said. "But I'm not planning to have it right away."

"Madam getting rid of her box. *Hayi, hayi, hayi.*" Lena sounded quite horrified.

"What's a box?" I asked.

"Where baby grow," Lena answered.

I imagined a shoe box in my mother's stomach.

"She means the uterus where the embryo grows into a baby," my mother explained. "Lena, don't say box. It's not very nice."

Lena tilted her head intently.

I wanted to ask how does the baby get there, but I knew she wouldn't say anything more elaborate than the father plants a seed there. I knew that. I wanted to know the secrets.

"I'm glad you're not having any babies," I confided to my mother, and with my finger I wrote an invisible but fervent message on my father's smooth bedspread: *Please, God, don't let my mother die.* Take the planting box, I prayed, but leave my mother.

4

Before she went into the hospital, my mother decided to invite the neighbors for dinner one Saturday evening. To ease her wifely duties, my father had suggested a sundowner rather than a full dinner, but my mother felt she owed them more than a drink and snack as they had welcomed her so warmly into their midst. She also felt that if we needed anything in her absence, they would be more willing to help.

Mathilda was cooking roast beef and chicken in ginger ale and soy sauce, and I was hovering around my mother, who was pouring brandy onto a swiss roll for the base of her spectacular, though seldom-made, trifle. She rarely went into the kitchen, relying mostly on Mathilda, but this was a special occasion. A spoon clattered onto the white enamel tabletop, and I knew my mother was thinking, "Too many cooks. . . ." Her nose started twitching and her scalp seemed to move as though irritated by an itch. "You make me drop things," she said nervously. "Go help Lena set the table."

Lena and I spread the crisp white tablecloth over the

dining room table and my mother came in to see if we were doing it right. "Chinese," she said of her best embroidered cloth. "One day I'll buy you one just like it." She was referring to some nebulous future when I would marry, which to her was the singular most important event in a girl's life. My aunt Phoebe had already started a "bottom drawer" for her daughter Ruthie, but my mother was too superstitious for that. She'd say things like, "Don't cross your bridges . . ." and "Don't count your chickens. . . ." I could have written a whole book on her superstitions, which in her case, may have had a sound basis: She had been single until her thirty-eighth year.

My mother set one place with her best cutlery and crystal glasses. She flicked a finger against one of the glasses so that it made a pinging sound, which she said was how you could identify fine crystal. Knowing those kinds of things was very important to people like my mother and Aunt Phoebe. Lena and I laid out the other places, making sure that the bottom of the silverware was one inch from the edge of the table. I used my thumb as a measuring stick. Then we rolled the linen napkins and stuck them very gently inside the water glasses so that they looked like many pairs of rabbits' ears.

"There's nothing more to be done right now," my mother said, after admiring the elegant table. "I just hope the guests get on well."

The neighbors were not too friendly to the only Afrikaans family on the block, but my mother found them charming and had been determined to include them in the guest list. "Besides," she had said, "having Afrikaans neighbors could be helpful someday." She thought Mr. Van Zyl Smit worked for the government, and he must be quite posh with that double-barreled name. I was quick to remind her that this was not England and that the Van-Zyl-whatevers didn't even speak decent English. Just as quickly, my mother countered that she liked to hear them speak the Afrikaans language, which had evolved from their Dutch and German ancestors, because it reminded her of Yiddish.

"You need to take a rest now, Liza, if you want to stay up tonight," my mother said.

I had no intention of taking a rest. Instead I followed Lena to her room in the backyard—forbidden territory—where I liked to listen to her stories of African devils, including the *tokoloshe*. Her heavy, iron bed frame was raised on bricks so that the little *tokoloshe,* who terrorized women at night, wouldn't be able to reach her in her sleep. The small room, which smelled of mothballs and her magic skin cream, was crowded with her meager belongings. A framed picture of her son stood on an old, wooden dresser. Her clothes hung from a rod behind a curtain, and berets of every color—some made of felt and others she had crocheted herself—dangled from a thin, wooden hat stand. These were for Sundays and her afternoons off, when she would dress up and scarcely wave good-bye as she rushed off to the bus that would take her to the township where she lived—that mysterious place where I was not allowed to go.

Although Lena was an adult, every time she went back to the township my mother would have to sign her pass book, giving her permission to come home after dark. Now I saw her pass book lying on the dresser, and she caught me looking at its yellowing, creased cover. I took a pencil and flipped the cover over, and there was a blurred picture, presumably of her, though it could have been of anyone. I closed the book with the pencil tip.

"That Dr. Firewood, he start all that. He want to treat us like children." Lena's voice rose angrily. I knew who Dr. Firewood was—she meant Dr. Verwoerd, the prime minister, whom all the maids hated and I despised because my father had said he was pro-Nazi during the war.

"Nothing ever change," Lena said. "You go now, *intombazana,* I must wash and dress for tonight." No doubt she wanted to take a bath before the evening chill set in, for her bath was an iron tub that she carried to her room and filled with buckets of hot water from the kitchen. Lena took down her favorite floral overall with its matching apron, and I went off to find the least hideous of my cousin Ruthie's hand-me-down party dresses.

As a spoilt only child, my cousin Ruthie had an extensive wardrobe of outfits that she rarely wore more than once. Thus, while Evie's well-worn clothes were donated to Israel, my aunt Phoebe gave to several charities—including me. My mother was fond of saying that those who give will always receive, and in the case of clothes I believed this to be entirely true.

The Frazers were the first to arrive—their first public appearance since their eldest daughter, Charlotte, had arrived home from college six months pregnant. Of course Lena had been the first to hear of Charlotte Frazer's condition. The so-called bush telegraph that operated in the countryside was even more effective in the city suburbs, where every house had a maid who, more often than not, was a confidant to her madam. Gossip ricocheted between maids' rooms like shrapnel from a cannon. Lena had also

31

been the first to know, even before the papers were signed, that an Afrikaans family was moving into the neighborhood, and that Mrs. Frazer had exclaimed to her maid Agnes, "What is this place coming to?"

My mother had laughed at that. "How quickly people forget their own beginnings," she had commented, referring to the fact that Mrs. Frazer had been a lowly shop girl who had managed to catch the son of a British peer in what my mother described as "a weak moment." But there was no denying that Mrs. Frazer was an adept student of the upper classes, for she soon learned to carry herself like a duchess, and spoke with a hot potato in her mouth.

"Hello, darling heart," she said as I opened the door. I didn't feel any special glow at being thus addressed—she called all children "darling heart" and adults were all "jolly good chaps." Preceding her husband into the lounge, she glanced around. "Well," she said, "I see the *plaasjaaps* haven't arrived yet."

"The what?" my mother asked, not understanding the Afrikaans colloquialism.

"You know, the country bumpkins," Mrs. Frazer explained.

"Now, Doreen," my mother said, "behave yourself. They're no more bumpkins than you or I, and I think he may have government connections."

The Johnsons arrived next, and then the Samuels with their son, Jeremy. Mr. Samuels walked slowly because he had a lot of weight to carry. He smiled and pinched my cheek, then made a joke I didn't understand because he came from the old country and was more fluent in Yiddish than in English. His wife, Sarah, was short and frumpish with fly-away gray hair. Mrs. Frazer didn't approve of her. I had heard her say to my mother, "That woman could buy

32

a farm in Main Street, and she walks around looking like a poor white." The Frazers didn't approve of Jews in general, but, like us, the Samuels were an exception. Mr. Frazer couldn't get over the fact that a man who couldn't read or write had managed to become "stone rich," as he described it, and still lived according to the Bible. The Samuels didn't flaunt their wealth, though they did live in the largest house on the block. Despite its impressive exterior, I never liked the big, dark rooms with their heavy mahogany furniture. Only when Jeremy played the baby grand did the atmosphere change. I would sit next to him on the tapestried piano seat requesting every popular tune I could think of, and magically, his long, pale fingers would press the right notes. I confided in Evie that some day I hoped to marry Jeremy, with his long, silky hair and burning-black eyes, but I realized that it was highly unlikely, as he had won a scholarship to a conservatoire in Paris and told me secretly that he hoped never to return. I dreaded the thought of never seeing him again, but Evie consoled me with the thought that he would at least return to see his parents. Evie agreed that he was quite divine but far too serious. She preferred fun-loving chaps like Harry Pollack, who was taking her out that evening.

My mother begged Jeremy to play "a little tune" on the piano, and Mrs. Frazer insisted that she wanted to see Evie dance. With everyone cajoling her, Evie finally kicked off her shoes, and pirouetted across the floor in an impromptu dance like some elegant bird of paradise. Jeremy watched Evie admiringly as his fingers skimmed the keys. And as the small audience applauded, I had a vision of Jeremy and Evie bowing and curtsying to thunderous applause and shouts of "Bravo!" in the great capitals of Europe.

The sound of Harry Pollack's special ring at the door

buzzed into my thoughts, and Evie quickly pulled on her high heels and grabbed her evening bag. "Bye everyone," she shouted breathlessly.

"Don't stop, Jeremy," my mother said. And his fingers changed rhythm from the delicate notes of Tchaikovsky to a more strident march.

"Do you hear what he's playing?" my mother whispered, as though it were of great significance.

Even I recognized the piece—it was Mendelssohn's wedding march.

When Mr. and Mrs. Van Zyl Smit arrived, the friendly chatter quietened down and everyone became terribly polite. I wondered what Mr. Van, as he said we should call him, thought of the tall, casually clad Jeremy with his longish hair, for the Van Zyl Smits were typical straight-laced Afrikaners, he with his hair cut short in the back and on the sides and his three-piece suit, and she with her homemade frock and sequined angora bolero to dress it up. Her tidy hair had probably been wrapped up like snails into pincurls all afternoon and the waves pinched into place with steel pincers. My mother broke the awkward atmosphere by ushering everyone in to dinner and boasting that I had set the table and folded the serviettes as though this were the greatest achievement of all time.

"My children help all the time," Mrs. Van said. "We don't keep a servant, and I tell the kids they must do things for themselves because one day all the Bantu people will be living in their own homelands."

"How on earth are twenty million Africans supposed to survive on thirteen percent of the most arid land in the country?" Jeremy asked quietly.

Before his question could penetrate, my mother cut in. "Oh dear, I hope they don't send our domestic help away

34

too soon! You should have seen what the women looked like in England—worn-out drudges, the lot of them. Of course it was wartime, so I suppose that had something to do with it."

"Tell us about the bombing," I urged, loving to hear my mother's war stories and sensing that politics was a taboo subject in this company.

"Oh yes, our house was bombed in London and my hair started falling out in clumps. I had to wear hats to work—crocheted them myself because there was no money to buy anything."

Like Lena, I thought.

Soon everyone was listening to my mother talking about her job in the Ministry of Supplies. She was so vivacious that I could see everyone loved her almost as much as I did.

"You know, I always tell Liza how lucky we are to have fresh fruit and vegetables. During the war everything was rationed and, would you believe, all the carrots were kept for pilots in the airforce. So you see, carrots do give you good eyesight . . ." she turned to me to finish her sentence, which I had heard many times.

". . . and curly hair," I filled in.

Everyone laughed as though I had said something terribly funny, and went on to talk about their children's bad eating habits. My mother looked around at the animated company with the satisfaction of a diplomat who had just defused an imminent catastrophe. Jeremy's question remained unanswered and seemingly forgotten.

When everyone had finished the hors d'oeuvres, my mother rang a little crystal bell to inform Lena that it was time to clear the table. Clearing the table and bringing in the hot dishes was Lena's job because Mathilda had worked hard in the kitchen all day. But Lena did not appear. Instead, Mathilda stood in the doorway and said, "Madam, I am needing to talk to you." My mother got up and I followed her into the kitchen.

"Lena is gone," Mathilda said. "She has not been here all evening."

My mother twitched with indignation. "How can she do this to me—tonight of all nights," she said fiercely. "Go look in her room, Elizabeth."

I walked out into the yard and knocked on Lena's door. No one answered so I tried the handle. The door creaked open and the smell of the mothballs and face cream overwhelmed me as I fumbled for the light switch. Everything was the same as it had been earlier—the photograph, the berets, and the pass book lying on the dresser. I went back to the kitchen and reported that Lena's things were in the room and she couldn't possibly have run away, because her pass book was there. I knew she would never have run away, but it was not uncommon for maids to quietly pack their bags and leave their places of employment without notice.

Mathilda said that while we ate the main course she would ask around the neighborhood. "Perhaps Lena out visiting one of the gels and forget the time," Mathilda said grimly, indicating that if this were the case, Lena would get a mouthful from her.

Everyone enjoyed the chicken and beef and asked for recipes, which pleased my mother no end. She was positively glowing when she rang the little crystal bell again. Mathilda appeared in the doorway and my mother told her how much everyone had enjoyed her cooking. Mathilda smiled and dropped her head like a shy child. Then she looked up and made a public announcement. "Madam, three gels they were talking outside an hour ago. They did not have their pass books, and the police took them in the back of their van."

I almost choked with shock. I thought of the hideous pass book on Lena's dresser, and I knew how the police, "those power-hungry, uneducated hoodlums," as my father called them, must have shoved Lena and her friends into their van with the dreadful metal bars. I had seen them roughly rounding up pass book offenders before.

"How could they take them from right outside the house?" I blurted out. My mother gave me a look that shut me up. She looked at the Van Zyl Smits and wailed, "These maids are so unreliable. What am I to do? Just when things were going so well!"

My mother had struck a chord with Mr. Van. "Unreliable, you are so right," he said. "Tell you what, I'll call old Potgieter at the station and he'll fix things up."

My mother drooled her thanks. She gave the others a look that said, See, I told you it was useful having Afrikaans neighbors.

Mr. Van made the phone call, speaking rapidly in Afrikaans. He returned to the table, enjoying the silence and his moment of importance. "They're there all right," he said. "We can fetch them after dinner."

My father and Mr. Van went to fetch Lena and her friends from the police station while my mother served coffee and I handed round After Eight chocolate wafers and truffles. When I heard the car brake in the garage, I ran out to see Lena as she walked through the yard to her room. Her pretty, floral overall was all crumpled. Her shoulders sagged and she didn't look at me. I should have run out to give her a hug and say it was all right, but the truth was I couldn't bear to touch her. She'd been contaminated by being in jail. My mother came into the kitchen and took out the food that had been put away. She piled a plate high and poured a large mug of sweet coffee and took it out to Lena's room.

It was late and I was tired, but I went back into the lounge. I had no intention of going to bed until the last visitor had left. The conversation had dwindled, except for Mr. Van and Jeremy, who were talking about the conservatoire in Paris. "Yes," Jeremy said, "I don't plan to come back. There's no future here. Tonight just proved that."

As my father said later, "You could have heard a mosquito breathe in the ensuing silence," but at the time he had a stricken look on his face as though expecting to have to quell an argument.

Then Mr. Van spoke again. "I agree with you, Jeremy. These kaffirs will never learn their place. Mind you, Verwoerd knows how to put his foot down—if anyone can teach them a thing or two, it's him. Ah, Verwoerd, now there's a man!" He popped a truffle in his mouth and smiled as everyone watched with fascination as he chewed.

5

My mother said that my father carried the whole world on his shoulders. If he wasn't worried about the political situation (his party never won elections), he would worry about the stock market. Or the horse races! The "inside" information gleaned from jockey acquaintances seemed especially fabricated for outsiders. Now, with my mother in the hospital, my father's brow was perpetually furrowed. Sometimes I counted the creases and decided there was one for each problem.

Although my father's concerns had always seemed remote to me, my anxiety about my mother's hospitalization matched or even surpassed his; but Evie, who had previously enjoyed sharing my father's confidences, showed no sympathy for him at this time. She flippantly declared that a lined forehead made him look old, and that marriage obviously disagreed with him. It was hard for me to be around Evie these days since she was so obviously happy to be in charge of the household again. In fact, she had become so tolerable since my mother's hospitalization that her temporarily shelved boyfriend, Harry Pollack, was hanging around again and she sang incessantly, "I'm just crazy 'bout Harry and Harry's just crazy 'bout me," until I was ready to choke her.

In a burst of energy, Evie completed the sweater she'd knitted for my father and presented it to him on a Saturday morning, the third day after my mother's operation. The gift was wrapped in the brown paper that Tilly stored away to drain her fried fish. *For my favorite Pop-sicle,* Evie wrote in her large, round hand, and to please her, Father tried on the sweater right away.

"Daddy, you look so handsome in your new sweater," Evie crooned, straightening the shoulders. She patted his slightly rounded belly. "There, it's a perfect fit. Go look in the mirror."

"Thank you, darling," Father said abstractly, kissing her lightly on the forehead. I could tell he was anxious to leave, to visit my mother in the hospital before seeing his Saturday morning patients at the surgery.

"Come on, Daddy," I nagged. I was eager to leave, too—to see my mother for the first time without her "box."

"Wait, master!" Lena came puffing up with a carrier bag. "This food for Madam. Hospital food too terrible bad."

I wondered how Lena knew about hospital food. Everyone knew that Provincial Hospital was for whites only. And then I remembered that my natural mother must have been in the hospital for a long time, and Lena had experience in such matters.

"And Beauty, she make some biscuits for the madam—in here." Lena pointed.

"But Lena, you made them! I saw you making them

yesterday when Tilly was off. Don't give us that Beauty rubbish," Evie exclaimed.

"Miss Evie wrong." Lena frowned at her, then turned and looked me straight in the eye. "*Intombazana,* you tell the madam Beauty make the biscuits for her. And master, please tell the madam she must get better quick. We are missing her too much around this house."

Evie looked at Lena from under half-closed lids, her top lip raised in a sneer. Her look was partly of disgust, but it also contained an element of disbelief. I, too, couldn't help wondering about Lena's sincerity, for since my mother's absence, she had spent the mornings chatting on the telephone to friends, and every afternoon the neighborhood maids had congregated in our yard, where she provided them with tea and slabs of bread with jam. She had even borrowed cups and saucers from our everyday set when there weren't enough enamel mugs to go around. Lena would never dream of insulting her guests by offering them tea in one of Cuthbert's empty jam tins.

Our next-door neighbor, Mrs. Frazer, had called several times about "the jabber" permeating through the fence during her siesta time, but I loved to hear the maids talk. Their loud, vehement voices overlapped in the still afternoon air, the emphatic clicks of the Xhosa language lending great import to every statement. Lena must have given several detailed, gory accounts of my mother's operation, because between the unfamiliar words, I heard "madam" and "box" repeated several times. Her audience sat riveted as her hands slashed the air, wielding an imaginary knife, and her mouth grew ugly with the horror of it. Although every maid appeared to have an anecdote about her madam, Lena's story, received with the loudest cries and

41

clucks, was undoubtedly the hit of these afternoon sessions. How unlike the chatter of my mother and Aunt Phoebe, who drank tea with their pinkies elegantly crooked and spoke in low voices about the latest marriages and divorces and their most recent servant problems.

"Well, are there any more messages for the hospital?" my father asked, turning hopefully to Evie. But she was busy getting his hat out of the hall closet. Either she didn't hear or she pretended not to hear.

"Here's your hat, Dad," she said, perching the gray felt on his head and planting a good-bye kiss on the tip of his nose, just like my mother did every morning.

"Come on, Liza, let's go," my father said, digging for his keys in his jacket pocket. "Do something useful with yourself today, Evelyn," he called over his shoulder.

Outside, the emerald-green kikuyu grass sparkled thickly with dew. I pulled open the sodden, wooden gates to the driveway and thought of my mother lying in a stuffy hospital ward. She loved the early mornings and could stare indefinitely at the trees and sky and even into the heart of a single flower. Nature, she said, contained the essence of honesty and beauty, and she alone understood when I pointed to the faces in the clouds and saw waves crashing in their ever-changing patterns.

My father reversed out of the driveway and I climbed onto the leather seat, which was icy against my bare legs. "I wonder how your mother's feeling. I wish Evie would open up to her more—she's such a good woman and loves you girls."

He didn't expect an answer. It was as if he were talking to himself, but I couldn't resist a little spite.

"Oh, Evie's just jealous," I said, "and by the way, that

42

sweater she knitted looks a little lopsided. I would give it to Cuthbert if I were you."

It was too late. I had said it and I should have bitten my tongue instead.

"You are not me and the sweater is very nice," my father replied sternly. "Besides, it's the thought that counts."

The hospital corridors reminded me of school, with their lime-green and cream walls and disinfectant smell. I held my breath so that I wouldn't breathe in any germs, and by the time we reached my mother's ward, I was almost in need of resuscitation. I felt suddenly shy and froze in the doorway, wondering how this pale, frail figure lying in bed in a pink nylon bed jacket could be the same person who, until just a few days ago, had been the pillar of strength in our household.

"Liza, how wonderful to see you," the pathetic figure said, extending an arm, but still I didn't move. "Is that parcel for me?" she asked. I was carrying Lena's parcel of food.

"Lena sent this and she said that Beauty made the biscuits, but I know she didn't. Evie and I both saw Lena make them. She just wants you to like Beauty better than Tilly." My voice was shrill with embarrassment and indignation.

"Liza, tell Lena and Beauty thank you, and the rest will be our secret. I assure you that, in any case, the biscuits would not affect my feelings for Beauty or Mathilda." My mother's low, controlled voice made me feel foolish.

"Is that a new sweater, Abie?" she asked.

"Yes, it's the one Evie knitted."

"It's absolutely stunning. Tell her I think she's marvelous with her hands."

43

"Don't you think it's lopsided?" I muttered, hoping to recruit my mother as an ally, but she apparently didn't hear.

"What else is news?" my mother asked, looking at my father, but I rushed ahead, and she gave him a smile and a look that said, He who hesitates is lost!

"Lena has been talking on the phone nonstop, and Mrs. Frazer has called twice to complain about the noise in the afternoons," I volunteered.

My mother sighed. "Mrs. Frazer doesn't understand like we do, does she?" The natives' loud speech, my mother had once explained to me, was a carryover from the time when they lived in the countryside, where they had no telephones and would shout to one another across great distances.

"These poor people are so controlled as it is, can you imagine if we also tried to control the volume of their speech! Heaven knows what they would do out of frustration!"

I knew that my mother was referring to the national cliché that every white family could expect to be stabbed to death by the next-door maid.

There was a knock at the door and a nun's face appeared.

"Ah, we're disturbing you!" said a voice with an accent just like my mother's.

"No, no, come in and I'll introduce you to my family," my mother said, sounding pleased.

Three nuns filed in, filling the tiny room with their flowing black robes.

"Sister Katherine, Sister Josephine, and Sister Therese—they're also from Ireland"—my mother smiled— "and they've been to visit me every day."

"We're from Dublin, too," Sister Katherine said, and they all nodded happily.

"And they've promised to come and visit us at the house," my mother said, her voice becoming weaker, as though our presence was beginning to tire her.

I groaned inwardly at the thought of the nuns visiting our house. Fiona Frazer would never believe that my mother was Irish-Jewish.

"I have a friend at the Holy Rosary Convent school who plans to be a nun," I said. "Her name is Megan, but she says she's going to be Sister Magdalena. Her mother is so proud, but my mother would die if I didn't get married."

Sister Katherine's wrinkled face creased into a smile. "Ah, but your friend will be married—to the Lord, that is."

"Will she have to shave her head?" I asked, unable to detect any wisps of hair escaping from under the tight, white border of the nuns' black veils.

My father coughed. "We need to be on our way; your mother is tired and I have a lot of work to do." He kissed my mother and whispered something to her. "It's been nice meeting you," he said to the nuns, giving a small bow in their direction and slightly raising his hat.

"Little Liza looks just like you," the youngest nun said to my mother as we were about to leave.

I looked back at my mother with one eyebrow raised in a question mark—a gesture learned from my English teacher to indicate her disapproval of young ladies who spoke out of turn. But my mother just winked at me.

"Thank you, Sister," she said graciously.

6

"Why are people so stupid?" I asked my father. "That nun must know Mom is not my real mother, so how can she say we look alike?"

"She was just trying to be kind, or maybe she really doesn't know. Anyway, I'd rather have people who are stupid and kind than stupid and vindictive like some of my patients."

My father was angry with some of his white patients who had complained about his not having separate surgeries for blacks and whites. At great expense and discomfort, the old house on Caywood Street, where he had practiced for years, had been renovated to accommodate those who favored separate facilities.

"Anyway, the complainers are paying for this renovation nonsense," my father said, grimacing. Then he grinned gleefully so that his eyes popped. "What they don't know is that I have only one instrument sterilizer for all the instruments, and anyway, you can't write *blankes* and *nie-blankes* on stainless steel!"

My father's policy was to charge his patients according

to their means, so that while his wealthier white patients paid according to a semistructured fee scale, his black patients often paid only a few pence.

What my father found interesting, he said, was that no black person ever wanted charity. It was a matter of pride to pay in full, even if it took several months.

"Of course, if I had my life over," my father said, as he often did, "I would be a farmer."

"Maybe I'll be a dentist, then I can help you."

"Heaven forbid!" He looked horrified. "Why would you want to deal with Mrs. Baskind's halitosis, or Uncle Sid's ropy saliva, or Mr. Glazer's shrinking jaw?"

We cruised slowly down Caywood Street, which was steep and curved, and as my father pulled up to the curb in front of the surgery in his shiny, blue Studebaker, I felt like arriving royalty. The verandah surrounding the old house teemed with natives, most of whom were swathed in blankets, and almost all had scarves covering their mouths so that only their dark, enigmatic eyes were visible. They had bussed or walked from the township or the surrounding countryside, and at least one had arrived by donkey, a mangy-looking animal tied to a street lamp in the alley separating the surgery from the next building, which housed *Die Oosterlig,* the Afrikaans newspaper and government mouthpiece. It often occurred to me that my father's black patients never owned cars, shiny or otherwise.

In the back room of the surgery, Popeye, the dental mechanic, was testing the bite on a set of dentures. A row of jaws in various stages of development, from white plaster casts to unnaturally pink gums sprouting pearly white teeth, grinned from the shelves.

"Hello *kleintjie,* you come to help old Popeye?"

We both knew I was no help, but more of a hindrance. I

had my own little corner in the workroom where I kept rubber molds in the shapes of various characters that I would fill with a plaster of paris mixture. When the mixture was dry, Popeye would help me peel off the mold, and presto! I would have an ornament to paint and glaze.

"I think I'll make this ballerina for Evie," I said. "It can be her going-away present."

Although everyone called Popeye by his nickname, because of his puffy cheeks that were like the cartoon character's, my father always called him by his real name, Mr. Coetzee, out of respect. Mr. Coetzee, my father said, was the best dental mechanic in the country, but he caused another furrow in my father's brow because he was unreliable. Like many Colored men, Popeye had a drinking problem that was caused, my father explained, both by a lack of identity and by the unusual circumstances of his personal life. The Colored people, descendents of white settlers and native women, considered themselves to be brown-skinned Afrikaners. Although they spoke the Afrikaans language and bore the names of their white forebears, they were regarded as second-class citizens and had even lost the right to vote. To complicate matters for Popeye, he had been educated in England and had married a white woman overseas.

For many years, the Coetzees had lived in South Kloof, a community of Coloreds, Indians, and Chinese, until the government declared the area for whites only. At that point, the Coetzees were legally divorced, so that Mrs. Coetzee and their son, Willem, who passed for white, could remain in the house. Officially, Mr. Coetzee was said to have moved to a Colored area, but I knew that he lived with his family in secret, because at the end of every month I would drive with my father to the little cottage in South

Kloof to deliver Popeye's wages to his wife. My father explained that this was to ensure that Mr. Coetzee was not tempted to drink away his earnings before his wife had paid the bills.

"So tell me a story, Popeye," I said, pouring the chalky plaster of paris mixture into the mold of a ballerina. Popeye loved to tell stories and I was a good listener.

"Once upon a time, when I was a young boy living in the country, we had an old, old teacher with a long white beard. It was so long that when he sat in a chair behind his desk the beard reached the desk top. In fact, he was so old that he would fall asleep in midsentence. His head would drop to his chest and he would snore till the bell rang at the end of class. Then he would jerk his head up and look around like a wild horse and shout, 'Dismissed!' "

At this point in the story, Popeye reached beneath his chair and took out a brown paper sack. He turned his back to me and took a quick swig from the bottle hidden inside it.

"Telling stories is thirsty work," he joked, in answer to my disapproving look.

I desperately wanted to stop him from drinking, to somehow make him so happy that he would never want to drink again.

"You know, Popeye, my dad says that with your hands, you'd have been the most brilliant dentist."

Popeye turned his slightly bloodshot eyes to me and I realized he'd already had more to drink than I had thought.

"*Ek meneer en jy meneer, wie sal dan die wa smeer?*" he said sarcastically in Afrikaans, and I recognized the expression from the list at the back of my Afrikaans Taal book: If I am sir and you are sir, who will then polish the wagon?

"That's your government's policy," he said, grimacing. "They believe some people are born to do menial work."

"You know it's not my government. I'm not a Nat," I said indignantly, not quite sure what exactly the Nationalist government stood for, but aware that my parents didn't vote for them.

"Anyway, don't you want to hear the rest of my story, *kleintjie*? OK, so one day when the old man's head fell to his chest and he snored so loudly that a draft blew through the room, we kids took a bottle of glue and stuck his beard to the table." Popeye slapped his leg and wheezed with laughter. "Then, when the bell rang at the end of class, the old man raised his head—*harumph, harumph*—he was stuck there!"

"What did he do, for heaven's sake?" I cried, thrilled at the idea of "getting" a teacher.

"We had to cut off his beard." Popeye turned around and took another swallow from the brown bag.

"We couldn't do that at our school," I said disappointedly. "All my teachers are old spinsters, though some do have mustaches."

Popeye pointed his finger at me. "The moral of the story is this: Don't get caught napping! Just like your Popeye who must always keep awake so that no one will see him sneaking into his own house or see him working here." His voice was so bitter that my skin tingled.

I knew that the workshop was out of bounds to visitors, and that if anyone were to have come snooping, Popeye always had a broom handy and would pretend to be the cleaning boy. My father said that no one would be happy to know that their dentures were made by a Colored man, and I wasn't even sure if a Colored man was allowed to hold such a responsible job.

"D'you think my ballerina is dry?" I asked, taking the

mold down from the shelf. "I think I'll paint the skirt pink. Evie likes pink—she can put it in her room at the university."

Popeye took the rubber mold from me and ran it under the hot-water tap. Then he gently peeled the rubber from the white figurine, revealing pointed toes, a tutu, and arms crossed in front of the bodice.

"My boy is also at Wits University, you know."

Of course I knew. He'd told me a thousand times about his brilliant son, and I didn't want to hear about him again. All I wanted was for the ballerina to come out in one piece, and the narrow neck was the difficult part.

"He's a real world-shaker," Popeye said, leaning down for another swig from his bottle. He looked around furtively and whispered, "He's in the Movement, you know."

"What's that?" Now I was also whispering, sensing that this was a very secretive exchange.

Popeye took another gulp and started laughing so hard that he had to sit down.

I was growing nervous. Who was this stranger laughing so hard at something I didn't understand? "What's so funny?" I asked, picking up the ballerina and easing the rubber mold over the neck.

"Oh no! The head broke off," I cried, stamping my foot with irritation. "All that work for nothing." As I squeezed the disconnected head from the rubber mold, it rolled onto the floor like a white marble. But instead of showing sympathy, Popeye was laughing so hysterically that he lay down on the floor wheezing.

"So many heads must fall," he gasped.

"You're drunk," I said disgustedly.

He lay crouched pathetically on the floor and openly

raised the bottle to his lips. He was no longer laughing, and his cheeks were wet. With his free hand he waved weakly at me as if to say, Go already! And as I was leaving, I thought I heard him whisper, "Go help your pa."

On the way home from the surgery my father was deep in thought. I stared out the window at the houses, which seemed to grow larger and their gardens more lush the further we drove from North End. Large double-storeys lined Cape Road, the main thoroughfare from the suburbs to the city, and on every block of the wide, busy street, bus stop shelters spilled over on the *nie-blankes* side with African women dressed in their finery for an afternoon off in New Brighton, the black township.

"I wonder if Lena's there," I said, scanning the crowd, which had become an angry, fist-raising mass as yet another full bus passed by. I knew how mad Lena became when the buses were all full and she had to spend her little free time waiting at bus stops. When I was younger, Lena would take me to town by bus and she would say, "Those bus conductors are making me so mad, *intombazana*. You see how empty it is downstairs where the white people sit." But I didn't like to sit where the white people sat. It was so boring. Everyone sat tight lipped and stared at everyone else, while at the top of the narrow, spiral staircase a different world awaited me—a world of sweat and old perfume, where every inch of space was filled by gesticulating bodies and vigorous voices jabbering in Xhosa. Close to the ceiling were signs I used to read aloud, mispronouncing the Afrikaans, which Lena translated for me: *Nie-Blankes,* meaning "nonwhites," and *Moenie spu nie,* meaning "don't spit!"

"*Moenie spu nie,*" I said aloud.

"What's that, Liza?" My father looked puzzled.

"That's what it says in the buses—*moenie spu nie!*" I realized that I had never known my father to ride in a bus. "Maybe you should put one of those signs in your surgery," I said.

"On the contrary, I'm always telling patients to rinse and spit! But you know what I don't understand about these African women? They keep asking to have out a healthy front tooth—just one, mind you—and when I refuse, they say they'll have it done elsewhere."

"Oh, that's a love gap," I said. "Lena has one." Although I spoke like an authority on the subject, I had no idea of the real significance of this strange practice.

My father took his eyes off the road and looked at me in astonishment, as though seeing me as someone other than his "baby" for the first time.

"Dad, what is the Movement?" I lowered my voice as Popeye had done.

My father's eyes narrowed and he sucked on his bottom lip so that the corners of his mouth turned down. "I don't know, and I don't want to know." Then his voice grew a little kinder. "Look, my girl, stay away from Mr. Coetzee. His problem is getting worse . . . *tsk, tsk, tsk.*" He clucked his tongue and shook his head. "I've done what I can for him. Even sent him to Alcoholics Anonymous, but the man is a difficult customer."

"You told me yourself Popeye's problem is not entirely his fault. You're just changing the subject because you want to keep secrets from me. Now what is the stupid Movement?" I badgered.

"It's an illegal organization that opposes the Nationalist

53

government, and the Nats have ways of dealing with these people. So now we need never discuss this again, since no one in our family is politically inclined and that's the way it's going to remain."

And from the look on his face I knew the conversation was over.

7

Mathilda was retired from her job as cook at the end of January, on the same day that Evie left for Witwatersrand University in Johannesburg. In the general upheaval of getting Evie ready for her new life, my twelfth birthday and new seniority as a standard-five student had gone almost unnoticed by my family.

Mathilda shed tears of joy and sorrow—sorrow at leaving the household, but joyful that my parents had provided for her retirement. "To be sure, this old body will have good rest, *intombazana,* then your Mathilda will be back," she said, grabbing my shoulders with her calloused, eagle hands and shaking me gently.

"Of course, Mathilda, you must pay us a visit any time," my mother said pleasantly on hearing Tilly's plans, but her emphasis on the word *visit* made it quite clear that Tilly should not think of her return as a permanent one.

"You wait, *intombazana,*" Tilly giggled, showing her yellow teeth and making her gurgling bathwater sound. "Your Tilly will be here to bake the next birthday cake—

yo, yo, yo! Not too long now and this little one going to be big teenage gel."

I shuddered at the thought. Already my body was out of my control. Tiny breasts had started to bud, making contours in my shirts, and I was developing round shoulders trying to hide this new phenomenon from the world. "Please God, please don't let my breasts grow until I'm at least fifteen years old," I prayed daily, as I stared in the bathroom mirror in a state of fascinated horror. When no one was watching, I had acquired the habit of pushing my palms against the unwanted buds in the hope of stunting growth. I had even thought of binding my chest as the Chinese did their feet.

To add to my self-consciousness, Evie had given me two parting gifts: A cute pair of frilly tennis underwear and—horror of horrors—a beginner's bra. That's what it said on the box in big, blue letters: BEGINNER'S BRA. I could feel my face flush crimson and rushed to hide the unspeakable thing at the very bottom of my underwear drawer. Never would I wear that thing, especially not with the bra-mania at school, where everyone was running their fingers down everyone else's back to see who was or wasn't wearing one.

"Darling," my mother said at lunch as we ingested Tilly's last overcooked chicken and three lifeless vegetables, "developing is a natural thing." She and Evie exchanged looks, and for the first time since our new mother had arrived, I felt like the outsider. I realized that they were probably in cahoots and had bought the bra together since I had refused to go shopping for one. I swallowed my last bite, shoved away my plate, and ran to my bedroom, hoping that my father hadn't heard all that talk about developing.

On my bed was the cricket set my parents had given me for my birthday. I ran my hand along the smooth wooden bat and thought of Delia's face when she had heard what I'd wanted for a gift. "You're such a tomboy," she'd said despairingly. I envied Delia, who had no problem about developing.

"Come sit on my suitcases," Evie said, standing in the doorway of my room. "Otherwise I'll never get them closed."

We went to her room, where a trunk and two large suitcases gaped open.

"Why d'you need so many clothes?" I asked.

"Oh, it's my university trousseau. Lydia says it's the most important time of a girl's life. She says this is the time to catch a husband." Evie giggled. "She's crazy."

"What about Harry?" I asked.

"Oh, Harry's OK, but he's not for me. Lydia says I should set my sights higher. After all, I'm going to get an education and Harry's going to be working in a jewelry store for the rest of his life."

Since when did Evie listen to our mother? I was amazed.

"Well, to tell you the truth, what Lydia says about Harry doesn't count. It's just that I've found him kind of boring lately."

"But Evie, you're always singing that you're crazy 'bout Harry."

"For heaven's sake, Liz, that's just a song, and anyway, people's feelings change. I'm sure Harry has dates lined up for every day of the week. Here, help me write these suitcase labels, and then I'll be ready to leave."

The train station was crowded with students going off to the university. Evie's friends had just as many suitcases as she did, so I gathered that my mother's philosophy was not unique.

"Look, Dad." I nudged my father. "There's Popeye. I'm going to say hello."

"Elizabeth, you stay with us." But as I ran off, his words were swallowed by the din of excited young people.

"Hello, Miss Liz." Popeye scratched at his cuticles, apparently ill at ease as he stood a little apart from his wife and son. He was cleanly shaven and his wasted frame was enveloped in a dark, funereal suit. "Willem," he said to his son, "this is Dr. Levin's youngest."

Willem held out his hand and gave mine a firm shake. "Just as pretty as Pa said." His eyes pierced my skull and I didn't feel like he was talking about my appearance. If anyone else had made this comment, I would have retorted with Delia's favorite remark: Flattery will get you nowhere. But Willem's manner left no room for coy arguments. His self-assurance amazed me. He was short like his father, but the resemblance ended there, for he was stocky and well built like a rugby player, and his dark hair, sallow skin, and hazel eyes were a striking combination. I had never seen a Colored who looked or acted like him. But why did I think of him as Colored? His mother was white and he passed for white. I blushed at my own thoughts.

"My sister's also going to Wits," I said quickly, covering up the guilt that no one else knew about. "Come say hello." I hesitated then, wondering if my family would want to meet the Coetzees in public. After all, my mother was constantly reminding me that my father was "a somebody" in the community and who we children associated with reflected on the family name.

"That's OK." Popeye hung back as though reading my thoughts.

"Sure, I'd like to see the doc again," Willem said, not at all bashful and leading the way toward our group.

"You've grown into a handsome young man," my father said, shaking Willem's hand. "My daughter Evelyn is also going to Wits this year. I hope she does as well as I hear you have."

Willem looked at Evie and then at her luggage. "You going to get an MRS degree?" he asked in his guttural accent, a relic of growing up in the impoverished South Kloof neighborhood.

She blushed at his sarcasm, and I realized it was the first time I had seen Evie speechless. She just stared at him.

"What charisma," Evie breathed, as he left.

As the train belched its first warning, we huddled around Evie.

"Remember, Evelyn, it's always important to look nice, and also, be choosy about your friends," my mother said, cramming in some last-minute advice. "And most importantly, stick to your own kind." My mother's expression was deadly serious. "Otherwise it will kill your father."

Whenever Evie or I did something that my parents disapproved of, my mother would accuse us of "trying to kill your father" or "taking years off his life," at the very least. At first I used to watch my father anxiously to see if he would keel over and die, but later I realized this was merely one of my mother's neuroses. However, I truly believed that our bad behavior would subtract years from his life, and thus I always calculated our misdeeds in terms of months and years.

The train lurched, and Evie and her girlfriends shrieked. My father looked depressed, and my mother's face was grim as she dabbed at her eyes. I wondered if she was still dwelling on her belief that Evie had the power to adversely affect my father's health or whether she was genuinely sad to see Evie depart. I decided it had to be the latter. After all, Evie's power "to kill" my father would surely diminish with the miles between them.

8

Evie had been gone for more than six months, returning only briefly during her midyear vacation. Beauty, meantime, had moved into Tilly's old room—a temporary move, my mother had insisted, until we found a more experienced cook, but it soon appeared that Beauty had become a permanent fixture. I was surprised that Lena hadn't moved into Tilly's lighter, airier room, but she chose to keep her old room, which had a good view of the backyard and, hopefully, of unwanted intruders, who were becoming a problem.

Three clocks had disappeared from the kitchen windowsill over a period of months, and Cuthbert had complained about garden tools missing from the shed in the backyard.

"Look here, Lena, Beauty will have to go." My mother's voice was agitated. "She's attracting all the riffraff of the neighborhood. We just can't have these *tsotsis* coming into the back yard like this."

"Madam, Beauty is a good gel. You know I tell these *tsotsis* to *hamba voetsek!*"

"I know you do your best, but you can't be a policeman either," my mother argued. "Maybe we'll just have to put in a gate, then the only way to Beauty's room will be through the garden, and no *tsotsi* will want to risk being seen by one of the family and reported to the police."

Beauty shuddered at the mention of the police, as she still didn't own a pass book, which would allow her to work in the city legitimately, and even on her afternoons off she would often stay in her room.

"It's a pathetic situation," my mother said. "That young girl is like a caged animal, and she's only seventeen." But, at the same time, I wasn't sure just how hard my mother was trying to get her a pass.

Although I felt vaguely sorry for Beauty, my emotions were concentrated in another direction—Brian Johnson, our fourteen-year-old neighbor, who barely knew I was alive before my parents bought me the cricket set. Most of my waking hours were spent thinking about Brian's sandy hair, freckled nose, and lean, brown legs, and my school books were covered with his initials.

Because Brian loved cricket, I became an even more ardent fan of the game, and an afternoon game of cricket on our lawn soon became a tradition among the neighborhood crowd. At halftime, Beauty would bring out glasses of Oros and a plate of Marie biscuits, and often she would watch the game from the sidelines until, one day, as captain of a team, I invited her to play. There was a short moment of discomfort as everyone looked at everyone else, but from then on, Beauty was accepted as one of the players.

Beauty was a good batsman. She had more strength than any of the other girls, who were much younger, and sometimes she would swipe the ball across the fence and into the golf course, automatically clocking up six runs for her team. Her "sixes" made up for her rather slow gait at other times as she ran from base to wicket and back again in an effort to make as many runs as possible before the wicket keeper could receive the ball and catch her out of position. When Beauty ran, Brian didn't do much good as a fielder. He watched her as earnestly as I watched him, his eyes mesmerized by her heavy, swaying breasts and buttocks that rose and fell in a rhythm special only to African women, and that no amount of practice would ever enable me to reproduce.

We were in the middle of a game one afternoon when Delia rode up on her bike and sat with one leg planted on our front wall. "Hello there, yoo-hoo," she shouted. She pointed to Brian behind his back, then folded her hands over her heart and threw back her head in a mock swoon.

"Come and play," I yelled.

"Thanks, I prefer to be a spectator." Delia was still disgusted at my owning a cricket set, which she declared to be decidedly unfeminine. "Anyway, it's going to rain soon." As she spoke, the first few drops fell.

"I'll wait for you inside," she said.

"Yes, you may melt," I called out, wanting Brian to notice how sturdy I was and that a few drops of rain were not going to deter me. But as the sky grew darker, the rain began to pelt down.

"Our team to bat first next time," Brian shouted as everyone took flight.

I ran inside to join Delia, while Beauty hurried to the washing line to collect laundry before it got soaked.

"You'd better change your shirt," Delia said, "or your mother will have a cow. You know how she is about your catching cold."

"My mother's not here, but OK, just wait for me." I

was far too shy to let even my closest friend see me undress; although, at some point after noticing Beauty's charms, I had stopped praying to God for delayed upper-chest development, and I had finally removed the beginner's bra from its secret hiding place in my tallboy.

When I returned to the porch, Delia was listening to the radio and Beauty was dumping a basket of damp laundry in the corner next to the clotheshorse. My skin prickled almost to a blush when I realized that I had run for shelter without a thought about helping Beauty. She was drenched and her clothes were plastered to the voluptuous curves of her body. I expected her to be sullen, but she still smiled, accepting her duties without question or expectations.

"Go and change, for heaven's sake!" My voice sounded imperious.

"Wait, wait! Beauty, teach us the dance you showed us the other day," Delia cried.

Beauty smiled and began to sing what sounded like, "*Asisi noma thetha, hayi ya geza. . . .*" Her body swayed with the rhythm of the song and her head jerked back and forth like an inquisitive chicken's. Grabbing my hand, Delia sprang to her feet, dragging me with her. Beauty's hips gyrated and her shoulders heaved sensuously, but however hard we tried, we couldn't duplicate the flowing movements of Beauty's body. Delia and I were a mass of knobbly knees and jerky shoulder blades.

"Hoo, hoo, hoo," Delia hooted, stamping her feet like a spear-bearing warrior in the introduction to British Movietone News. "Come on, Beauty, show us how they dance in the tribal lands. I've seen them in films—the women are bare on top."

"Show us your titties, Beauty!" Delia and I were pulling at Beauty's wet shirt. But she was laughing and needed

64

little encouragement, and I was thrilled and disbelieving that anyone could be so natural and unreserved about her body. Her smooth brown breasts were large and firm and had a damp sheen either from her sodden clothes or from the exertion of the dance. The porch had grown steamy from our energy and the earlier sunlight that had been trapped in the many-windowed room.

Beauty rolled her bare shoulders and her body vibrated to the words that came from deep in her throat. For a moment she looked up and broke her rhythm. Delia and I caught our breath, but with eyes downcast, Beauty resumed her gyrations in a wonder of sensuality and muscle control.

As Beauty reached the end of her tribal dance, our dance also came to an end. Delia twirled me around, and in that instant I caught sight of a face in the misty window. It was a human fish with bulging eyes and open mouth. Sandy hair clung like seaweed to the startled face of Brian Johnson.

"Oh Dele!" I whispered, "I think I'm going to die. Brian saw us and he's going to think I'm absolutely crazy and disgusting."

"There's nothing wrong with dancing." Delia smirked.

"But what about Beauty—she'll be so embarrassed."

"I think she knew he was there all the time," Delia whispered. "In fact, I think she was dancing for him." She giggled. "You saw him watch her outside, didn't you?"

I squirmed. "You are quite revolting," I whispered indignantly. Sometimes I really wondered about the grotesque thoughts that crowded Delia's head.

Our cricket games gradually fizzled out after that afternoon. Beauty was becoming overweight and sluggish and I even heard my mother telling Lena not to overfeed that young girl—it was unhealthy. Lena laughed and said that *indoda* liked their women with some meat on their bones and that Beauty would soon be ripe for marriage. When I knocked on Beauty's door in the afternoons, she smiled, revealing a newly acquired love gap in her front teeth. Her voice sounded sleepy and she often made the excuse that she was resting. Eventually I didn't bother her anymore.

9

Like Noah's animals about to enter the ark, the standard-five class stood in line, two by two, ready to march to assembly for the last time. Next year we would be entering Queen Victoria High School, situated in a formidable building across the street, but for the moment, we still had to endure our last day as juniors. From across the courtyard we could usually hear the strains of "We Are Marching to Pretoria" or "Onward Christian Soldiers," but today the chatter was so intense that it all but blocked out Miss Henshaw's voice booming, "Come come now, girls! You can talk about your plans for the summer holidays later on."

"Six weeks of bliss," Delia squealed, taking absolutely no notice of Miss Henshaw's admonition.

How Delia had changed in the seven years at Queen Vic, I thought. When we had first entered the sub-A class at the age of six, Aunt Rebie had driven us to school every day in her long, black limousine, which she drove as regally and slowly as the queen's carriage. Inevitably late, Delia would start blubbering as soon as we turned onto

Bird Street and came to a stop outside the school building. My feelings for my closest friend were ambivalent. Although I wanted to comfort her, the urge to be on time was greater. Perhaps, at this time, I was more compelled than most to do the right thing, since many of the teachers knew who I was. To them I was Evelyn Levin's little sister, or "Levintjie," as the Afrikaans teacher called me, using the Afrikaans diminutive attached to my last name. They often asked after my sister Evie, but before I could ever reply, they would purse their lips or suck in their cheeks and say things like, "That was a character for you" or "What a little devil she was." Although these remarks were said with affection, I was careful not to live up to Evie's reputation.

Now, as in years past, we marched to assembly with our backs upright, our shapeless, pleated, navy tunics tied neatly round our middles with a girdle and our navy and white striped bowties pinned to our white shirts. "Left, left, left-right-left," we whispered to ourselves out of habit, but no longer dreading that we would "wrong-foot" and feel Miss Pelham's ruler at the backs of our knees, for surely at this stage we were impervious to her wrath.

Miss Pelham, the headmistress, was short and trim, with a voice that could fill the city hall without a microphone. Her enormous, red-veined eyes were terrifying and missed nothing. In assembly we stood in rows staring up at the podium, where she sang loud and clear, drowning out our rendition of "The Lord Is My Shepherd" and turning it into an aria. When our lungs had been duly aired, Miss Pelham regaled us with reminders to wear hats and blazers in public places—even on the last day of school— and to remove school colors and emblems from old uniforms passed down to the children of "African employees." Miss Pelham would never use anything as indelicate as "servants." Finally, she wished us a happy holiday, and the entire school responded by shouting as they did every year, "No more pencils, no more books, no more teachers' dirty looks!"

On the bus home from school, Delia asked if she could come over for the afternoon, but I quickly made an excuse. "I have a tennis game," I lied, not wanting her to meet Evie's new friend, who was spending an inordinate amount of time at our house.

Evie had already been home a week for her summer vacation, and she was a very different person from the one who had left home almost a year before. Her interests had changed from boys and clothes to a passion for politics. She and my father argued incessantly, so it was a relief when she made plans to go out in the evenings.

On the way home from the bus stop, I stopped several times to lay down my heavy school case. Besides, the longer the walk took, the longer I would be away from the situation at home. As soon as I reached the corner of Allen Street and Westview Drive and saw Mrs. Johnson's pinched smile and heard her curt "Good afternoon," I knew that Willem Coetzee—Popeye's son—was visiting Evie again.

My father had forbidden Evie to see Willem, but she retorted that she refused to have him choose her friends for her, and if he didn't want Willem in the house because he happened to have Colored blood in him, that was fine because she would go to his home in South Kloof instead. My father was silenced and my mother turned a blind eye when Willem visited in the afternoons, never mentioning to my father how much time Willem was still spending at our house.

As I walked up our driveway, my suspicions were confirmed. Willem's bike rested against the hedge. I went to my room, changed into shorts, and laced up my *takkies* to practice tennis outside against the wall. I could hear Willem and Evie talking and laughing in the porch. They always talked incessantly, especially Willem, who seemed to me like a teacher exploding with knowledge and wanting to teach his favorite pupil everything he knew in as short a time as possible.

I had been hitting the ball against the wall for a while and was concentrating on a backhand when I heard Willem's voice. He and Evie were out on the lawn, and I realized they had probably been watching me from the porch window.

"I hear you're playing in a tournament in two weeks."

"Uh huh."

"Look *kleintjie,* I don't want to interfere, but if you want to win, you got to do more than *bloop* the ball back and forth. Tennis is like life—you got to go after what you want." If he hadn't given me a dimpled grin and said it with a twinkle in his eye, I might have told him to take his advice elsewhere.

"You see, if you go *bloop,*" Willem continued, arcing his finger through the air, "there's a ninety percent chance your opponent will also go *bloop*"—another arc—"so you must cut off her *bloop* at the net with a *pow!* Here, let me show you."

Willem took my racket and hit the ball against the wall. As it rebounded, he ran forward and smashed away a volley.

Evie smiled and clapped, but I remained sullen, determined to show no sign of friendship. "I can't do that!"

"You can do anything you set your mind to," Willem said severely. "If we can find a tennis court, I'll be your coach for the next two weeks, and just see if you don't win that tourney."

His enthusiasm was contagious. In spite of myself, I could feel a sudden charge of adrenaline. "The Queen's Club is down the road, and no one plays there during the week. You can borrow Evie's racket and we can ride down to the courts now." I hoped I didn't sound too keen.

"Ride!" Willem scoffed. "Your sister can ride; we're going to run. Don't think I'm going to be easy on you—tennis is not just hitting the ball; it's moving fast and having the stamina to stay out there as long as it takes."

Willem ran at a leisurely pace, but I sped off down the road as fast as I could, determined to show off my agility. After a few minutes, I was gasping for breath and had a fearful pain in my side.

"That's your first lesson," Willem said, slowing down to walk with me. "You have to pace yourself, otherwise you won't last out a match."

We worked for an hour on volleys until my muscles ached and sweat dripped onto the court. He had worked as hard as I had, but wasn't even breathing hard.

"When did you first start playing tennis?" I asked.

Willem looked at his watch and frowned. "Since about an hour ago." Then he laughed delightedly at my look of astonishment.

Every afternoon for two weeks I practiced with Willem. I no longer cared about the looks from the neighbors or the nasty comment from Mrs. Frazer, who said she thought Evie's friend looked like he had more than a touch of the tar brush. My parents were delighted that I was keeping Willem away from Evie, and she, having grown bored with the tennis scene, spent more time with her "normal" friends, as my mother called them.

71

My first match of the tournament was on a Tuesday afternoon, and on Monday, after practice, Willem asked what my plans were for the following day.

"I guess I'll go to the beach in the morning with Lucy," I said. My cousin Lucy was visiting from Vereeniging and we went to the beach every morning with the driver my mother had employed for the summer.

"Tell me, Miss Levin, how do you usually feel when you come home from the beach?" Willem spoke as though he were a doctor questioning a sick patient.

I thought for a moment. "Thirsty, I guess."

"What else?"

"Pretty lazy. Ready for a nap."

"And this is how you want to feel when you go into your match tomorrow?" There was a slight edge to Willem's voice.

"You have made your point. I will stay home and do nothing."

"Not nothing. You can hit against the wall. If I weren't working I would hit with you in the morning, but I hope to get off in time to see the match."

He must have seen the horror register on my face. "Please don't watch—it'll make me nervous. I don't even let my parents watch my matches." This latter remark was true, but it wasn't the reason I didn't want him to come. I couldn't bear the embarrassment of Evie and Willem being seen together in front of the tennis crowd at the Davies Stadium. And there would be a crowd—all the top stars in the country would be playing in the open division.

"You're a nice one," Evie said to me later. "You're willing to take what you can from Willem, but not to give him the pleasure of seeing how much he's helped you."

72

"Oh girls," my mother interjected, "don't bicker. Your aunt Phoebe called and asked us over for Shabbat dinner on Friday night. She's having a large crowd and says it's important that we all come."

The anticipation of a large family gathering washed away my guilt about Willem. I loved family get-togethers, perhaps because I was the youngest and rarely had a chance to spend time with my older cousins. But, by the time Friday evening arrived, I had changed my mind about Aunt Phoebe's dinner.

"Mom, I'm not going tonight," I said, as I watched her brush her hair and dab cologne behind each ear.

"Is that so? And why not?" I saw her eyes widen in the dressing table mirror.

"The final is tomorrow afternoon and it's just too important. I must have an early night."

I had won four matches in the girls' fourteen-and-under division to reach my first final in a major tournament.

"Darling, you can sleep late tomorrow! Tennis is wonderful for fresh air and exercise, but you don't want to get so serious about it."

"I am serious, and I cannot go," I said firmly, irritated that my mother could never understand my passion for the sport.

"That Willem must be some motivator," my mother said, shaking her head.

Before everyone left for the evening, my mother, Evie, and I lit the Sabbath candles and said the Hebrew prayer, but I silently added one of my own: God, please let me win tomorrow.

I sat in the darkened dining room in the flickering candle-light. Friday night was always my favorite time to sit and dream until the Sabbath candles burned themselves out, but tonight my mind was a tennis court where I played out every point of a two-set match, winning by the amazing score of 6–0, 6–0. Even as I sat in the dark, I could feel the smile of victory touch my lips, but it quickly faded as I realized how lonely it was with no one to share my success.

The house was so quiet I could hear the silence, broken only by the ventriloquists of the night—crickets shrilling outdoors. I went to the telephone in the hall.

"Willem? This is Elizabeth Levin."

"What's the matter, *kleintjie?*"

"I'm in the final. It's at two o'clock tomorrow."

"I know, *kleintjie,* I went to the stadium and looked at the draw and also saw your opponent play."

"What do you think?"

"Man, I think that girl's as big as an ox—strong, but can't move. You just move her all over the place and do your *pow* shots and she'll be a dead ox!"

"D'you think I'll win?" My voice sounded childish, even to my own ears.

"*Kleintjie,* remember I told you you can do anything you want?"

"Yes, I remember." My voice was stronger now. "I just beat her in my head in two love sets."

Willem laughed. "You see, it's a fait accompli!"

"A what?"

"Forget it. Is your sister there?"

"No, she's gone to a family dinner."

"You didn't go?"

Maybe he didn't believe me that Evie was out.

"No, I wanted an early night before my match."

"*Kleintjie,* if that's your attitude, you've already won in

74

my book." Willem sounded as delighted as if I had given him a gift.

"Willem?" I took a deep breath. "Will you come to my match tomorrow? I'd like you to be there."

"Huh? You think I'd miss the match of the season?" He spoke without hesitation, as though he'd been planning to come all along. "Listen, if you get there early, I'll warm you up."

"It's a deal!" I said.

When I replaced the receiver, I felt a sense of calm. The clashing crosscurrents of my mind were all flowing in one direction, and sleep came easily to me.

Sometime during the night, I was wakened by a babble of voices and smothered laughter. My mother was whispering to Evie and Cousin Lucy to hush, then she tiptoed into my room and peered at me in the dark.

"I'm awake," I said croakily. "What happened?"

"Such excitement," my mother whispered, as though she didn't quite believe I was awake. "Your cousin Ruthie is engaged to be married."

"What! To that drip she's been dating?"

"Selwyn's a nice boy, in spite of a bad accent, and your aunt Phoebe says his family 'knows how to live.' "

"Does that mean he's rich?"

"They're in the underwear business," my mother said, as though that would surely answer my question. "Everyone has to wear underwear!"

My father stood in the doorway. "Lydia, couldn't the news wait till tomorrow?"

"I was awake, Dad, really."

"It could be Evie getting engaged if she just showed some interest," my mother said with a sigh.

"Please, Lydia, you want her married at the age of nineteen to some schlemiel with no education?" My father's voice was sharp. "Come, let's leave Elizabeth to sleep before her big day tomorrow."

Saturday afternoon was blustery, and only the center courts were shielded from the wind by the grandstand seats rising to a deceptively calm, blue summer sky. Our match was relegated to an outer court exposed to the elements. After almost two hours of battling both the wind and my opponent, the score was one set each. We stopped for a short break, and I paused at the fence where Willem sat watching.

"It's impossible," I panted. "She kills me when I serve into the wind. I've got no energy left."

"You sure as heck got more than she does. Just take a look."

My opponent was sitting down next to her parents with her shoulders hunched and her legs splayed out, and her face was a steaming red.

"You got to lob to her backhand," Willem said, "especially when she's against the wind. Then you come in with the volley. Also do your ugly little drop shots when you're against the wind."

All these things to remember! I started off badly, but then my opponent went into a slump and I caught up. We battled back and forth until the score was four games all. My opponent was serving badly now, and choking on easy shots. We changed sides at five games to four in my favor. Again I was serving into the wind—this time for the match. We patted the ball back and forth, each waiting for the other to make an error. "Deuce," I called out, as I finally hit the ball in the net. Maybe it was my turn to go into a slump! As

76

I returned to the baseline to serve, I saw Willem's hand shielding his eyes as though he had a headache.

Gosh, this must be so boring for him to watch, I thought, as the cheering from the center court arena filtered through. I knew that at this point in a match a great player would take charge, and I decided to do just that. The very next point I followed my serve to the net and so startled my opponent that she made a weak return and I was set up for an easy winning volley. I looked at Willem and he gave me the thumbs-up sign.

"Add in," I shouted, buoyed by my latest tactic. I served to the add court, planning to come to the net again, but my ball was several inches out. My opponent returned the serve into the net and began to walk toward me with her hand outstretched. She obviously thought the serve was good and that she had lost the match.

"My serve was out," I shouted to her.

"You sure?" she asked.

I nodded.

"Take two," she said.

I served again, and she went for a winner down the line, but it landed a few inches out.

Willem clapped and congratulated us both, and when the other girl left he stood looking at me with his hands on his hips and his dimple just visible in his cheek. "Interesting finale!"

I knew he was referring to the last point. "You know we were out there for three hours?"

"Don't tell me: I should have brought a sun hat."

"I couldn't just take that last point; I had to win it."

Willem patted me on the back and looked up at the sea of white faces watching the match on center court. "If everyone had a conscience like yours, this country would be a darnsight better place," he said. "Maybe tennis will eventually be your passport to get out of this godforsaken land."

Why did he and Evie have to relate everything to politics, I wondered. Why couldn't they be lighthearted like everyone else?

"You go phone home while I watch center court," he said. "Your folks must be on tenterhooks to hear the result."

My parents arrived with Evie and Cousin Lucy in time for the awards ceremony at six o'clock. When my name was called out, I walked up to the podium, remembering not to grab the silver cup before shaking hands, just as they had taught us at Queen Vic. As I returned to my seat, I could see my family smiling and cheering, and I thought how little they actually had to do with my victory. The one person who should have been there to share the credit was nowhere to be seen.

I didn't see Willem again during the remaining weeks of the summer holiday. On a trip to my father's surgery, Popeye mentioned that his son was working full time during the day and studying at night. I couldn't help but wonder whether my father and Popeye had something to do with his busy schedule.

10

Evie was back in Johannesburg, and peace once again reigned in our household. She never wrote to us about boys or dates, only about the terrible regime under which we were living. Then, as if to prove her point, at the end of March, hundreds of African protesters were killed or wounded during a peaceful demonstration outside the Sharpeville police station. A note of hysteria crept into her letters and she declared her conviction that only the Movement could save the country.

Our family in Johannesburg seemed to take delight in reporting to us that Evie was looking a mess these days and no one could discuss anything rational with her. These tidings added to my father's already overflowing bag of worries. He sighed heavily at the mere mention of Evie's name, but my mother made light of the matter, pretending that there was nothing to worry about. To me she confided that Evie was "killing her father," but all the while she reassured him that it was just a phase and to be expected.

She wrote letters to Evie about the dinner parties she and my father had attended, the latest news of Cousin

Ruthie's wedding plans, and tea-party gossip Aunt Phoebe had told her (and everyone else) in the strictest confidence. She referred to Aunt Phoebe as the CNA (short for the Central News Agency), which she knew would evoke a chuckle from Evie. She also told Evie not to spare any expense to look nice. She needed to make regular trips to the hairdresser and to treat herself to a manicure every now and then. And how was she enjoying the gorgeous clothes they'd bought together? I loved to read my mother's letters, which ran on without punctuation, just the way she spoke.

Evie ignored the questions, but she did say that she would appreciate the extra money offered to keep herself looking well groomed. She also wrote that living in residence was despicable and that she and her best friend, Sara, had found a house to rent that would cost my father no more than the residence fees. It would also be a place for the family to stay if and when they came to Johannesburg. *My entire happiness depends on this move,* Evie wrote dramatically, and after endless discussions at the dinner table, my father reluctantly agreed, although my mother called him a softie.

"Oh, well, Sara Kahn sounds like a nice girl and probably comes from a nice Jewish family," my mother said, sighing and acknowledging defeat.

A house in Johannesburg sounded wonderful to me. A few of my very wealthy school friends (whose mothers wore long gowns to dinner every night) had summer houses in Plettenberg Bay, and now we would have a second house in Johannesburg.

"Please, please let me stay with Evie when I visit Lucy in Vereeniging," I begged. Every winter vacation I visited my Levin relatives on their farm outside Vereeniging, about an hour's drive from Johannesburg. "I could stay with the Levins for two weeks instead of three."

My father smiled at me indulgently as if at a week-old infant. "You're my baby," he said. "I'm not letting you go to Johannesburg with no one to look after you."

"But Evie will—I promise, I promise!"

"You know, Abie," my mother said, "it might be a good idea. Liza could tell us firsthand what's going on there, and it would give Evie a sense of responsibility. Maybe that's what she needs."

My father's expression was not happy, but I could see that he would reconsider.

"So it's settled. I'm going, I'm going, oh boy!" I ran outside and hit a tennis ball against the wall until I was exhausted. Throwing the racket down on the grass, I sprawled out on my back under the winter sunshine. The grass was prickly and alive with a world of activity beneath my skin. Maybe the bugs beneath me had a city—a city like Johannesburg that hummed along at a breathless pace. The sky floated above in shades of clear blue with wisps of white clouds smoothly merging and falling apart like partners executing a familiar dance. But when I closed my eyes, there were no shades of color, just plain orange. I wondered whether blind people also saw orange when the sun shone down on their eyelids, and what about black people. Maybe I would ask Beauty or Lena. I thought how Lena used to scare me when I was little by rolling her eyes back in her head so that only the blood vessels showed. I heard myself say "Ugh!" But another faint sound made me sit up.

Getting up so quickly made me momentarily dizzy and the garden looked dark and secretive.

"Brian, Brian, is that you?" I could make out his

stooped figure at the hibiscus hedge that separated our two houses. I hadn't seen him for ages and my heart was pounding unnaturally. I walked over to him. "Gosh, I didn't know there was a hole in the hedge."

He turned red.

"Did you want to play cricket?" I asked, trying not to sound too eager.

"Nah!" He hesitated a moment. "Thought you may want to fly my plane at the pond on the golf course."

Brian was a whiz at making model boats and planes he could sail and fly by remote control, and I was over-whelmed by the unexpected invitation. He climbed through the hedge and I followed. As I glanced back, I saw Beauty standing at the window of her room.

"Maybe we should ask Beauty to come with us," I said, knowing that I would be in serious trouble if my mother knew I'd been on the golf course without an adult or at least a group of children, and Beauty seemed the perfect solution to this problem.

"Nah, forget it," Brian said sharply, and I didn't argue or he'd think me a scaredy-cat.

Brian's room was a gallery of model boats and airplanes. We stopped long enough to pick up the equipment and then crossed the street into forbidden territory—a forest of long grass and pine trees riddled with mosquitoes and other flying insects. The pond was in a clearing quite a distance from the fairway, but not far from a tin shanty where the caddies lived.

I watched and admired Brian maneuvering his boat through the water and his plane through the air, but after a while I became bored and nervous. Not for a moment could I stand still without slapping at another mosquito biting my leg or a dragonfly diving past my head, and I wondered if Brian noticed how my glance kept straying toward the tin shanty.

"Please could I have a turn," I begged for the umpteenth time.

"OK, I guess," he said grudgingly, handing me the controls.

For a while I forgot the insects as the plane rose and dived and undulated under my direction.

"That's far enough. Bring it back now," Brian demanded. The plane was close to the tin shanty, and a few dark faces appeared in the distance, watching the puppet plane.

"How do I do it?" I was losing control.

"That knob to the left, silly." Brian was shouting now.

When the plane nosedived to the ground, I knew I had pushed the wrong button. Brian's face was white and then flushed red with anger as he screamed, "You allowed the plane to crash! How could you do that?"

"Allow! Gosh, I'm sorry. I didn't do it on purpose." I was whimpering like a baby and hated myself.

"Go get it. Get it right now!"

"I'm not going to get it. You know I can't go over there."

"You're afraid of *tsotsis*," he said, sneering.

"You're just as afraid, that's why you won't go yourself," I shouted, turning in the direction of home and trying not to run like a baby. I felt a sharp jab at the back of my head and heard something hit the ground. My hand went to the painful spot and I could feel blood oozing onto my fingers. Now he was pelting me with stones and I ran in terror through the tall stinging nettles and the dark shadows of the trees.

The half-mile walk stretched to infinity, and when at

last the row of familiar houses came into sight, I climbed through the wire fence without the slightest caution and into the full view of my mother, who was pruning shrubs in the front garden.

"Look at your face and legs scratched to pieces!" she yelled. "What happened?"

As soon as she was reassured that nothing serious had happened, she admonished me that terrible things could happen to young girls, and that next time the *tsotsis* would be waiting for me, and it would serve me right. And how could I expect to go to Johannesburg if I had no sense of responsibility.

Lena came out to see what the commotion was about, and I flung my arms around her. But she wasn't sympathetic.

"You listen to your mother very good, *intombazana*. Those *tsotsis* making big trouble. They supposed to be in school, but what do they do—they caddy on the golf course, they drinking and smoking and just looking for nonsense."

I buried my head in her starched white apron and mumbled, "But I wasn't alone, I was with Brian."

"Un-un-un," Lena said, shaking her head. "That young fella no match for *skollie* boys. *Tsotsis.*" Then she flicked an imaginary knife in front of my nose to show how the *tsotsis* dealt with intruders.

But I was no longer paying attention to Lena's dramatics. I had seen a movement behind the hibiscus—a flash of gray hair and the curve of Mrs. Johnson's tightly pulled-back bun. If she had been listening, I knew Brian would be in trouble. She took every opportunity to castigate him, and more than once I had seen her chase him around the garden, flailing his wooden cricket bat.

That night, after dinner, the doorbell rang, and I ran to answer it, thinking Brian had come to apologize. The front verandah was alive with flames. I slammed the door shut and streaked into the dining room where my parents sat, unaware that the house was about to burn. My mother followed me to the door and I stood back as she opened it.

"It's a paraffin fire—the kind that night watchmen use to keep themselves warm," she said calmly. "It's a prank, and you're not to play with that boy again," she warned. "His tricks are getting out of hand."

I could imagine Brian smirking behind the garden hedge. He must have received a mouthful from his mother, and this was his way of paying me back for blurting everything out. "Just like a stupid girl" was his usual accusation when I did something he didn't approve of. Perhaps he thought I told that he had struck me, and that may be why he never spoke to me again.

11

My mother arranged for me to travel to Johannesburg with Aunt Phoebe and Uncle Cyril, who were going up north to shop for Cousin Ruthie's rapidly expanding trousseau. Evie wrote that she was thrilled that I would be staying with her for a week.

The Colored driver from Uncle Cyril's secondhand furniture store took us to the station in the van because Aunt Phoebe had so much luggage. I was perfectly happy with the arrangement because it meant that not only would my parents be able to see us off, but Lena and Delia could come too. Lena had brought a bright red scarf and promised to wave it until the train was out of sight.

When Uncle Cy saw that Lena and Delia were coming with us, he muttered to my parents, "She's already a teenager. Can't she go anywhere without the nanny?" My parents ignored him. To me he said, "So y'shoulda brought the whole neighborhood."

Uncle Cy was not the sort of person you'd want to claim as a relative, but he had married Aunt Phoebe, who was my father's sister, so I had no choice but to call him Uncle. Now I wondered how I could possibly tolerate them both as my chaperones on the long trip to Johannesburg.

When we reached the station, Uncle Cyril jumped out of the van and struck a pose like the conductor of an orchestra until a porter ambled over to help with the luggage—a thin, sour-faced man in a black uniform and black, peaked cap. I guess anyone would have looked sour at the sight of Aunt Phoebe's profusion of suitcases and hatboxes.

Aunt Phoebe batted her eyelids at him and said in her soft, whispery voice, "You dear man, I've really overdone it, haven't I?"

"She's going to model for *Vogue*," Uncle Cy muttered to us.

"What's that, dear?" Aunt Phoebe asked in her you-dare-repeat-that voice. Delia and I exchanged looks and stifled a giggle.

Although a slow fifty, as my mother described her, Aunt Phoebe wore a girlish, pink floral frock with earrings to match. Her newly blonde hair was combed back in a chignon with just a few loose tendrils framing her lined face, and on top of this perched a pink straw hat, the brim of which appeared to be weighed down by a fruit salad. My aunt Phoebe liked nothing better than to be told that she and Ruthie looked just like sisters, and she did her utmost to maintain this youthful image. I had gleaned from family conversations that Phoebe was a good bit older than Cyril and she had married beneath her, but when you're a spinster and getting on in years, as so many hinted, marriage to Cy Saunders was apparently preferable to being left on the shelf. I had my doubts about this, though I had to admit Uncle Cy was a looker in his way.

His black hair was slicked back from his handsome, jowly face, and a thin, black mustache à la Clark Gable accentuated an Americanized accent adopted from films. His voice reminded me of the sea—kind of husky, and his *S*'s seemed to whistle. Even for the dusty train journey his clothes were up-to-the-minute—plaid trousers, a double-breasted jacket, and a white panama hat.

"Let's find the compartment," Aunt Phoebe said. Her lips were always rounded as though she were sucking on an invisible straw, and her eyes darted back and forth to the porter lest he leave behind any of her paraphernalia.

"On the turn," Uncle Cy replied.

The train stood at the platform like an impatient animal, snorting and belching steam. The engine drivers, their skin blackened with soot, shoveled coal into the engine. The cavernous station building was a hub of activity as vacationers started to crowd the platforms.

"Look at the talent," Delia whispered, nudging me in the ribs as a group of boys passed by. "Gosh, you're so lucky!" Delia was boy crazy and fell passionately in love with someone different every other week. I, on the other hand, was more steadfast, and still pined over the fact that Brian Johnson had turned out to be what Delia described as an "infantile pyromaniac."

The porter's trolley was stacked so high with Aunt Phoebe's luggage that Lena offered to carry my suitcase. I thought my father should carry it, but Lena had insisted, as though she needed an excuse to be there. I carried my school satchel, in which I'd packed books and a deck of cards to play solitaire on the trip, but I knew that most of the time I would stare out the window at the passing scenery or walk up and down the corridors peering in at other compartments and making temporary friendships.

I had packed my warmest winter clothes because the mornings and evenings in Johannesburg were frosty, and my aunt Rhoda was not one to turn on heaters. My mother had insisted I pack her own cashmere sweater, which had seen better days.

"If you slip your legs through the sleeves at night," she said, "you'll be warm as toast." That was a carryover from my mother's growing-up years in England and Ireland. She approved of whatever the English did. In fact, when the government expressed the desire to gain independence from Britain, her greatest concern was that English imports would be stopped. She had a horror of wearing locally made clothes. Whenever we went shopping she would look at the label first, and if it said MADE IN GREAT BRITAIN, she'd like it immediately even if it was quite hideous.

We found the compartment, and I swung myself up the tall iron steps and ran along the narrow corridor. The compartment was all shiny wood with green leather upholstery.

"I dabs the top bunk," I said.

"Of course, sweetheart, Uncle Cyril and I are too old to go climbing," Aunt Phoebe said.

"Speak for yourself," her husband shot back.

"Let's find the bedding boy," she said, ignoring him.

The bedding boy was a middle-aged Colored man who expertly flung sheets and heavy army blankets across the bunks, tucking the edges neatly away.

I loved my top bunk with its smooth, polished wood and glassed-in pictures of proteas and springbok. But best of all was the reading lamp, flush with the wall, which meant that I could read as late as I wanted without disturbing anyone.

The porter was still passing the luggage through the window, and Uncle Cyril was storing it under the lower bunks, on the luggage rack, and on the unused fourth bunk. I saw my father dig in his pockets to give the porter a tip, and I wondered why he would tip for the Saunders' luggage. Then I remembered my mother's description of Uncle Cy as thrifty beyond belief, but then she had added that maybe he had to be miserly to make up for what Phoebe spent on their daughter.

The train lurched and creaked. I leaned out of the window to kiss my parents. My mother dabbed at her eyes with a perfume-soaked handkerchief. "Do you have your spending money, darling? Buy whatever you want." I patted my jacket pocket containing the small purse of money I planned to spend on sweets and magazines sold at almost every stop. I held Delia's hand through the window as the train slid slowly out of the station.

"Have a *lekker* time," she said.

"Give love to Miss Evie," Lena called out, "and you be good gel."

Then the train was moving faster and Lena, Delia, and my parents grew smaller and smaller, and the red scarf became an almost invisible speck. Suddenly the world consisted of a maze of railway tracks and open space. Factories on the outskirts of the city gave way to fields lined with tangled acacia bushes. Clumps of yellow-orange aloes stood tall and bright in the winter sunshine.

The dinner gong sounded in the corridor as the "bedding boy" walked through the carriages from one end of the train to the other, knocking out a tune on the xylophone he carried.

"Da-da dee-dee tea and cof-fee," Aunt Phoebe sang as

the tune crescendoed outside our compartment door and then faded into the distance.

"Cy, dear, I have everything we need for dinner except tea. Please, could you order some from the dining car."

"The kid can go," he said. He always called me the kid.

"Thank you, Elizabeth." Aunt Phoebe smiled. "I'll lay out the dinner meantime."

To reciprocate for the Saunders' chaperoning duties, my mother had provided a dinner—chicken and cold meats, a variety of sandwiches, and fruit—that was sufficient to feed the entire train. Aunt Phoebe contributed one of her famous cakes that she always kept in case of guests. The cakes would grow moldy in their tins, but that wouldn't deter my aunt, who, when guests did arrive, would cut away the mold and serve the rest.

I lurched with the rhythm of the train to the dining car to order tea. Jumping across the narrow join from one carriage to the next was both exhilarating and terrifying. For an instant my hair blew in the wind created by the speed of the train, and down below, the tracks appeared like never-ending quicksilver.

"Hey chick, howzit? Where you going?" It was the group of three boys Delia had noticed at the station. I recognized two of them, Howie Bernstein and Morris Shapiro, from my trips to synagogue on Friday nights when Delia and I would dress in our finery and stare down past the edges of our prayer books and over the ladies' hats to view the "talent" downstairs. Because men and women sat separately, and because it was traditional for the women to sit upstairs, the boys would hold their prayer books up high, and occasionally we would notice someone gaze heavenward, pausing en route at our pew.

"So Lizbeth, come visit us later." I stared blankly at the third fellow who spoke. I had never seen him, yet he knew my name. "You don't recognize me," he said. "I live on Cape Road behind your house—Barry Kaliff."

My eyes opened wide. This gorgeous specimen with a shock of brown curls, high cheekbones, and a giant Star of David dangling around his sexy neck was the same person who, just a few years ago, Lena predicted would grow up to be rubbish because his wild behavior caused every nanny to pack her bags and leave within the first week of employment.

"Sorry," I gasped. "I haven't seen you in a while."

"Yeah, well, I guess we don't hang around with the same crowd," he said. His friends laughed as though they knew something that I didn't, and I blushed, wishing Delia were there. She would have known exactly what to say.

When I returned to the compartment, Aunt Phoebe had unfolded the table from the wall, and Uncle Cy sat with a napkin tucked into the neck of his shirt, filling his mouth with chicken. When he had gnawed every last morsel from its bone, Aunt Phoebe said, "Cy, dear, would you like a corned beef or egg sandwich?"

"Double or nothing," he replied.

She gave him one of each and I wondered at her ability to understand him. "Is there anything more you want, dear, before I clear away?" Aunt Phoebe asked.

"Potatis," Uncle Cy replied, and I gathered it meant he'd had his fill, because she started to wrap up the leftovers.

The adults retired early, and I wondered how they could sleep so easily. I could hear them snoring, and if I sat up in my bunk, I could see the glass of water containing Uncle Cy's dentures. Without teeth, he looked older than Aunt

Phoebe, his face all crumpled and his mustache crowding his chin.

I lay in my bunk reading, enjoying the beat of the wheels throbbing against the steel rails. The tune was constant, changing to a crescendo when the train crossed a bridge, and a muffled roar as it sped through a tunnel. The tunnels were scary, especially during the day, when we would be thrust into sudden darkness. At night the engine's shrill whistle would echo through the tunnel and the lights from the villages and farmhouses were shut out. Everyone would scramble to shut the windows, or else the entire compartment would be covered in soot.

I slept fitfully, waking whenever the train stopped at country stations. I could hear the babble and laughter of people and the creaking of luggage being passed through the windows and stowed away.

In the morning I awoke as the orange sun lit the landscape, which had changed overnight from green to gold. The lush vegetation of the Eastern Cape had given way to the dry grasses of the Orange Free State, still sparkling with frost. The farmlands formed a quilt of yellow wheat and brown soil. Sheep and cattle grazed peacefully, and clumps of mud huts with their thatched roofs broke the monotony of the fields. African children raced toward the tracks, raising cupped hands for food or a few pennies. The older children were dressed in tattered shorts and dresses, but the little ones ran naked on their skinny legs, which looked too fragile to hold up their empty but distended bellies.

I hurried to get some packages of fruit and sandwiches out of the cool bag and flung them out the window. I stuck my head out and could see the little African children flocking for the food like a flurry of pigeons scrambling for bread crumbs.

"Imagine living in a mud hut without a bathroom or electricity," I said aloud.

"That's what the natives are used to. They're happy as they are," Aunt Phoebe said.

"Evie says we shouldn't call them natives. They prefer to be called Africans. Anyway, how do you know they're happy as they are?"

"Gawd, the kid's becoming a commie," Uncle Cy interjected.

Aunt Phoebe gave him a look that stifled him. To me she said patiently, "They're not a sophisticated people." And her tone indicated that I had had no business asking her to explain.

"Here, next time give them the cake," Uncle Cyril said, "or there'll be nothing left for lunch."

After breakfast the train stopped at a dusty siding. Again the children came with their hands outstretched, the older ones with their flashing smiles and the little ones with their solemn eyes and runny noses. An old man, his skin wrinkled like the cracks at the bottom of a dry riverbed, held up some animal carvings he had fashioned from pieces of driftwood.

"Oh, Cy, isn't that delightful," said Aunt Phoebe, pointing to the image of a deer that had sprung to life under the old man's guidance.

"Five shillings, madam," the old fellow called out.

"Let me see it," Aunt Phoebe said, extending her arm through the window. He handed her the statue and she caressed the smooth wood with her manicured hands. "Just delightful," she said, "but on second thought, what would I do with it?" She held it out to him.

94

"You keep, you keep," the old man chanted, revealing his crooked, yellow teeth. "I give you for three and six-pence."

"No, no, I don't want it." Aunt Phoebe's voice had become shrill. "Give it back to him, Cyril." She sat down with her lips pursed.

Uncle Cy studied the wooden deer. "Hey, *indoda,*" (he prided himself on knowing some Xhosa words) "you haven't signed your name on it."

"You're not in a city gallery, Uncle Cy," I said. "He probably doesn't even know how to sign his name."

"Well, I'm not paying three and six for this," Uncle Cyril said. He reached inside the compartment for Aunt Phoebe's moldy cake wrapped in tinfoil. He handed it to the old man, who beamed and bowed his thanks, probably thinking it was a hunk of meat to feed his hungry family.

The train lurched, its segments jarring against each other like an uncoordinated caterpillar, and slowly glided forward. I couldn't believe it. There was the deer frozen in flight on the lid of the washbasin in the compartment. Uncle Cyril was sitting down. "You gave him an old piece of cake for this?" I was aghast.

"He needs it more than we do," Uncle Cy said, while Aunt Phoebe looked away, her face unusually pink.

I leaned out of the window and saw the children clamoring around the old man, wanting to pry open his silver gift shimmering in the sunlight. Filled with shame, I reached into the purse for the emergency money my parents had given me.

"Here," I shouted. "Here." I waved wildly and flung the coins through the window onto the receding platform. Clinging to the windowsill, I leaned out as far as possible into the wind, but the old man was already an imperceptible dot, almost indistinguishable in the dry landscape.

I left the compartment and went to the dining car, where I ordered a cream soda. The only other people there were a young Afrikaans family with six children under the age of eight, slobbering tea and cake all over the place. The mother didn't look the least bit anxious about the mess.

"The Afrikaners have children one after the other, like steps," Evie had explained to the family on her return trip from the university, "so they can swell the numbers of the white Nationalist population."

"Maybe they got the idea from the African people who do the same thing," my father had said.

"Well, if the African people weren't deprived of an education by the government," Evie shrieked, "maybe they'd know more about birth control."

I covered my ears at the memory of that awful visit, of Evie constantly arguing and crying and my father gradually withdrawing into a mute person I scarcely recognized.

"Hey babe, move over. What you looking so cheezed off about?" Barry Kaliff nudged me over and slid onto the seat next to me, while Morris and Howie sat opposite us.

"So what you got under that jacket you wearing?" Morris snickered.

I blushed, remembering that he had also been the one to scratch my palm when shaking hands and wishing me "Good Shabbos" after synagogue one Friday night. Delia had interpreted the sign in a whisper. "He's asking if you want to do it," she explained, almost spitting out the word *it*."

"Take no notice," Barry said now, not laughing with the others. "The guy's got zat culture. You hear that, Morris—

zat!" He got up and looked at the other two, giving them some kind of signal. "Listen," he said. "Me and this chick are going to take a walk. We'll see you later on."

I wondered if we were going to walk up and down the corridors all afternoon. That would be fine. I already had an overwhelming crush on this tall, handsome, assertive, newly found neighbor, so that all previous loves seemed as inconsequential as a raindrop in an ocean.

Barry didn't plan to do much walking. He opened his compartment door and said, "Come sit down." I obeyed and he locked the door and pulled down the shutters overlooking the corridor. I wondered whether I should lunge for the door, but instead sat nervously scrunched up on the green bunk.

"Listen, babe, get comfortable. I'm not going to bite." He spread his arms in a gesture of innocence. "You want a biscuit?—My ma baked 'em. My ma and pa are getting divorced, and I'm going to live in Jo'burg with my uncle for a while."

I gulped and almost choked on biscuit crumbs. Pictures of my wedding to Barry Kaliff, with Delia as bridesmaid, had flashed through my mind with prophetic clarity, and although my parents would be disapproving at first, they would finally come to love their son-in-law once he had had the tattoo removed from his arm. Now my dreams were shattered with this piece of information.

My expression told all, which is why my mother said she always knew how I felt without my telling her.

Barry seemed pleased at the effect of his news. "You gonna miss me?" he asked, as though we'd been seeing each other every day for years. "Listen, we can write, and I'll be coming back in the summers. We can go to the beach together and take some walks up Happy Valley."

Everyone knew what went on in Happy Valley, a park across the road from Humewood Beach.

"Why d'you have this tattoo?" I asked, pointing to a small, blue picture of a skull and crossbones on his forearm.

"That's my gang's symbol."

"What gang?"

"Duke's gang."

"Duke! You mean the king of the Ducktails?" Everyone knew about Duke, who was rumored to gate-crash parties and wear knuckle-dusters, which he would use if anyone got in his way.

"Sure, I hang around with those guys sometimes. Not all the time."

"You don't even have a duck's tail," I said, looking at his hair.

"Just takes a little Brylcreem," he swaggered, and took a comb out of his sock and scraped it through his thick hair. He edged a little closer.

"You got pretty eyes," he said, touching my lashes. "They'd be good for a butterfly kiss. You want me to give you a butterfly kiss?" He leaned over and fluttered his eyelashes against my cheek. I stopped breathing. All I could hear was a loud thumping coming from inside my chest, and I wondered if he could hear it too. Then he crushed his lips over mine like a wet suction. My mouth was shut tight and my eyes were wide open. Barry's eyes were closed, which made me think he'd done this before. In fact, he must have if he hung around with Duke's gang.

"Hey, babe, don't you French kiss?"

"Sure," I said, relieved. Finally I was on familiar territory. I had seen the French kiss in films and it certainly wasn't disgusting like all this wet, slobbery stuff. The

French knew how to kiss. They started with the back of
the hand and went all the way up to the elbow. I held out
my arm, but he ignored it. He was at my mouth again,
shoving his tongue between my lips. I felt his spit cold
around my mouth as his tongue darted inside. Then his
whole tongue was rolling around inside my mouth and I
had a strange, pleasurable sensation between my legs, as
though I were starting to wet my pants after holding in too
long.

"You a virgin?" he asked, coming up for breath, and I
wondered if it would look bad to dry off my mouth.

"No, of course not!" Virgins did it, didn't they? My
mind was in a state of confusion from the kissing and the
insult implied by his question.

"You wanna do it? Then we can go steady and I'll give
you this." He held the Star of David in his hand and pulled
it back and forth along its chain.

"No, I don't want to do anything, thank you." I spoke
coldly now, remembering my mother's advice that a boy
will offer you anything in exchange for your favors.

"You a little cocktease, you know that?"

"What's that mean?" I asked, but he didn't answer,
lunging instead for my mouth. This time I enjoyed the
sensation until I felt his hand creeping over my shoulder towards my breast. I caught his hand and withdrew
from him.

"I belong to the WHS," he said, sitting back with a
toothy grin and chewing on a piece of gum that I realized
must have been hidden in his mouth all the time he was
kissing me.

"What's the WHS?" I asked, feeling ignorant and out
of my depth again.

"The Wandering Hand Society. You want to become a

member?" He was still grinning when there was a rap on the door.

"I must be going," I said, guiltily patting my mussed hair.

Howie and Morris were at the door and stared at me as though I were a complete stranger. I wondered what Barry would tell them. I could have quite a reputation by the time I got back to Port Elizabeth.

"See you this evening," Barry said.

After dinner I wrote to Delia in the privacy of my top bunk: *Dear Dele, Boy have I got news for you. I am madly in love. . . .*

"Elizabeth, come have some coffee in the dining car with us," Aunt Phoebe cooed.

I put down the letter and combed my hair carefully. He could be in the dining car.

He was. He sat with his back to me, across from Morris and Howie, who grinned sheepishly when they saw me. Next to Barry sat a girl with hair teased into a beehive. He and the girl got up and I saw Barry give his friends the same signal he had given them earlier. The girl was at least sixteen, heavily made up with dark eyeliner and pale lipstick. She walked with small steps in her too-tight skirt.

"That's the Kaliff boy," my aunt said. "Has quite a reputation from what I hear. Not surprising with parents like that."

I hated her for saying that, and I hated Howie and Morris for sitting there like two accomplices. But most of all I hated myself for hoping that it was a big mistake and that Barry would return in a few moments.

That night I felt as though I had a large cavern inside me filled with the painful feelings of rejection, and, even

100

worse, a loss of self-esteem, but the feelings dissipated as I expressed them in a new letter to Delia. Besides, with the excitement of our impending arrival in Johannesburg after breakfast, I had no room left for bitter thoughts.

Beach-colored dunes from the gold mines flashed by the corridor windows as we reached the outskirts of the city. And a few windows down, I heard a young girl call to her brothers and sisters to "come look see the gold." It was Barry's girl with the beehive and she wore a large Star of David around her neck.

"Stick to your own kind," my mother had once warned Evie. I supposed it was good advice, but I wondered how exactly you could know who your own kind were.

12

Evie and her friend Sara met me at the Johannesburg train station. I saw them first through the compartment window. Evie had put on weight and her hair was unkempt. Her blouse hung loosely over her slacks as though she were trying to hide the added inches, and it occurred to me that the extra money my mother was sending her was not being used for its original purpose—grooming. Her friend Saraswathi Khanna was not Sarah Kahn of Jewish descent as my parents had thought. She was an Indian girl, very pretty with her long, thick black hair and black-fringed dark eyes.

When Evie caught sight of me leaning out of the window, she waved wildly and shouted, "Liz, Liz!" I returned her wave with less vigor because I was dreading the moment that Evie would bring over her friend and introduce her to Uncle Cyril and Aunt Phoebe.

"Look Phoebe, the kid's with a blooming curry-muncher," Uncle Cy said incredulously as he saw Evie hurrying along the platform to our carriage, and I knew that the news would be all over Port Elizabeth as soon as

Aunt Phoebe returned and had the undivided attention of her tea-party companions.

Sara shook hands with me and smiled with very white teeth when we were introduced, and she nodded politely at the Saunders, instinctively knowing not to offer her hand. I covered up the awkward moment by profusely thanking my relatives for taking care of me on the trip. Uncle Cy still looked positively stunned, so that my aunt had to remind him to give me a hand with my suitcase.

"Sara's car is parked outside," Evie said. "We can manage the suitcase ourselves." The old Evie would never have dreamed of carrying a heavy suitcase when she could have had a porter do it for her.

Sara had a little Austin, which she wound in and out of the heavy city traffic, past tall buildings and pavements thronging with people.

"We're coming into Hillbrow," Evie announced as we neared her house. Hillbrow was a maze of shops and foreign restaurants with names like Tony's Pizzeria and Venezia, and everyone on the streets looked Greek or Italian.

"Is this still South Africa?" I joked.

"It's exciting, isn't it? Very cosmopolitan," Evie said.

Her house was on a street of large, ugly, old houses with a thin strip of yard separating them. Inside was dark and gloomy and almost empty of furniture except for the beds in every room.

"I thought just you and Sara lived here," I said. "Why are there so many beds?"

"Oh, sometimes we have meetings here and they finish late, so people just stay the night. And we do have one or two semipermanent residents, like Sara's aunt, Mrs. Patel. Here, come and meet her."

Mrs. Patel nodded a silent greeting with her large,

round head. She sat immobile on a chair in the gloom, her brown sari exposing a tire of fat around her waist.

In her room, Evie had her old trunk and a narrow wardrobe that couldn't possibly have held the trousseau my parents had bought her.

"Surely all your clothes can't fit in this wardrobe," I said incredulously, yanking at the door and wondering why it wasn't open and spilling out Evie's usual mess. It was not only closed, but locked.

"Leave it alone. You'll unpack later," Evie said sharply. "My clothes fit in the trunk. I don't have many anymore. I gave a lot away to people who really needed them." She ignored my surprise and talked on. "We have to be at a meeting on campus in a little while, and it will be interesting for you to come along."

What else was I supposed to do, I thought. Stay alone in this mausoleum? So much for our holiday house in Johannesburg—it was the creepiest place I had ever been in.

Wits University was like a separate city of large, old buildings. Students were jammed together in the main hall, and the noise was like a wave that never fell. The boys were dressed casually in jeans, but the girls were neatly dressed in skirts and blouses, their hair teased to just the right height and their makeup carefully applied. They looked as I thought my mother would want Evie to look. A row of young men entered the front platform and a familiar figure stepped forward and raised his hand. A hush descended and I looked at the figure on the podium dressed in a blazer and tie. Although I had never seen him dressed so smartly, I knew instantly that it was Willem.

"You remember Willem Coetzee?" Evie whispered. "He's head of the student body."

"Of course," I whispered back. No wonder Popeye was

so proud of his son—a young man who could command attention by just raising his hand.

"Before we proceed with this meeting, I would first like to welcome our honored guests." Willem's voice was filled with sarcasm. "Sergeant Van Tonder and Sergeant Kleinhans of the Special Branch have honored us with their presence once again."

"Boo, boo! Kick them out, kick them out!" the students jeered.

"They come to every meeting," Evie whispered, pointing out two men older than the rest and dressed in sports jackets. "That Van Tonder is a real bastard."

I looked at the man with the stony, pock-marked face and greasy, blond hair. "Why don't they camouflage themselves by dressing like the students?" I asked.

"What do they care! They have the power behind them, and they think we'll be careful what we say if they're in the audience."

The jeers died down and Willem continued.

"Your student council has called this meeting to protest the banning of Professor Eksteen for reasons not given by the government. Professor Eksteen is being detained illegally without recourse to a fair trial." Willem's voice had grown stronger with that final sentence and he delivered each syllable like a retort from a gun.

A roar rose from the students. "We want justice, we want justice!" They chanted on and on as though they would never stop.

Finally, Willem raised his hand and again there was quiet. "Perhaps Sergeant Van Tonder and Sergeant Kleinhans will come away from this meeting with some knowledge of the rule of law, which they can then pass on to a government that denies its existence."

The students applauded their approval and Willem continued. His words floated over my head as I looked around me. The students were listening with rapt attention, and Evie, too, was under Willem's spell. But the two Special Branch sergeants fidgeted and looked at their wristwatches. Van Tonder opened his mouth in a wide yawn like a crocodile about to swallow its prey.

Then it was over. I stood with Evie and Sara as the students filed out of the hall. Willem came up to us. "So the Port Elizabeth contingent is here," he said, smiling at me. "See, you're never too young to protest." Then he gently squeezed the muscle in my forearm and exclaimed, "Hm, *kleintjie,* I can tell you're still slaying them on the tennis court!" I grinned shyly, overwhelmed by seeing Willem in his capacity as a student leader. He turned to Evie and patted her on the behind. "See you girls tonight. The meeting's at nine, and have something good to graze. I'm sure everyone will be hungry."

He spoke to Evie with such familiarity that I gathered she was still seeing Willem against our parents' wishes. "What's Willem talking about?" I asked her.

"Oh, there's a meeting at our place tonight. It will be quite late, so you can just go to bed."

"It's not a school night," I huffed.

"Yes, well, I'll introduce you to everyone and then you can go to bed." Evie was quite firm. She turned to Sara. "What shall we make for them?"

"Curry and rice, maybe?" Sara said, shrugging.

I had no idea my sister could cook. She had certainly never lifted a finger to help in our kitchen at home.

Sara found parking in Hillbrow and we walked to a grocery store with a sign that said Q. L. Son Hing above the door. The store was dark and smelled of old wood and exotic spices. A Chinese girl named Venus served us and took us to a back room where the wooden floor creaked with the weight of large barrels filled with grains, dried legumes, and spices. Venus measured a little of this and a little of that on a scale, according to Sara's instructions. Evie paid what Venus described as wholesale price, and she included a strip of licorice, "for the little sister," from one of the glass jars filled with sweets on the front counter.

We stood outside the store for a moment, blinking in the unexpected sunlight.

"Hello girls, what you doing here?"

"Oh, hello Chandra, we could ask you the same question," Evie said. "By the way, this is my baby sister, Elizabeth. Liz, this is Ramachandra."

Chandra was a tall, handsome Indian fellow. He shook my hand vigorously and introduced us to his friend Asan, who nodded deferentially as if he were not used to meeting white people socially. I knew how he felt. People around us were staring.

Chandra spoke again in his typically Indian accent, emphasizing the consonants and slightly slurring his vowels. "Up the road, I saw a car parked and I recognized it as belonging to the one I intend to marry." He looked innocently at Sara.

Sara had been standing slightly behind Evie and me, and I noticed that she had not uttered a word, but stood with her eyes downcast, her long lashes shadowing her cheeks.

When they were gone, she turned to us with her eyes dancing. "Isn't he just too handsome and wonderful!" she cried.

I looked at her in amazement. "But you didn't show the slightest interest in him," I said.

"Oh, but I couldn't. Things are different in the Indian community. If you look at a boy straight in the eye, people think you are flirting and you get a bad name."

"Well, we wouldn't have told anyone, would we?" I looked at Evie.

"Yes, but what about Chandra's friend," Sara said, "or even someone passing by on the street. That kind of news spreads like wildfire in the Indian community. Everyone knows everyone else's business. And it would bring dishonor to my family, especially to my father, who is very highly respected in that community."

I couldn't help smiling at the similarity between her community and ours, despite the difference in color. Listening to her talk was almost like hearing my mother say, "And always remember your father is a somebody in the community."

Sara took my smile for mirth. "You shouldn't laugh at another person's beliefs," she said. "You European girls are too forward."

I blushed at the thought of Barry Kaliff—of his wet kisses and how he had ignored me later.

"Yes, and what have you been doing?" Evie asked, my shame apparently glaring her in the face.

"I smooched with someone on the train." The words came out in a rush before I could stop them. I'd been wanting to tell Evie all day—to hear her say that I wasn't a harlot. But now, looking at Sara's shocked expression, I thought how lucky the Catholics were that they could confess privately and anonymously.

"You are only thirteen," Sara mumbled.

"Almost fourteen. But I could just die," I said. "I'm so disgusting. I'll never do that again."

"Yeah, till the next time," Evie mocked. "Look, don't

be silly," she added, "you're normal. Just so long as you don't go any further than kissing."

"Oh, I wouldn't! I won't!" I said, relieved that she knew of my infamy and had set boundaries within which I could conduct myself.

"Have you ever kissed Chandra?" I asked Sara.

"No, we have only met in the presence of a chaperone, but we have held hands. Oh, but the desire is so strong!" She winced at the thought of it, and then laughed at herself when she saw the empathy on our faces.

We had been walking all this time and now we entered the butcher shop, where Evie took charge and ordered what she needed. Sawdust covered the floors and carcasses hung from the ceiling on wire hooks.

"I think I'll wait outside," I said.

"Not in Hillbrow, you won't," Evie retorted.

"I'll stay with her," Sara said. And to me she said, "I don't eat meat, so to look at it raw makes me ill."

We stood outside on the pavement watching the shoppers pass by, but it soon became apparent that Sara and I were objects of curiosity. A European girl standing together with a sari-clad Indian girl was obviously a strange combination even in Hillbrow. If I had been with an older black girl, everyone would have accepted that I was out shopping with the maid. Sara was sensitive to my discomfort, and we were both relieved when Evie finally appeared.

At the house we helped Sara's aunt in the kitchen. As an antidote to the hot curry, we filled side dishes with sliced bananas, mangos, coconut, and chutney.

"Mrs. Patel, this curry is wonderful," Evie raved, taking a spoonful. The old lady smiled for the first time. "Go on, try some," she said, handing me a spoon.

I dug out a spoonful of the aromatic vegetable curry, and as soon as it was in my mouth I knew I had made a mistake. Tears poured from my eyes and flames enveloped my tongue and palate. Even my aunt Phoebe's homemade horseradish on Passover, to remind us of the bitterness of the Jews' slavery in Egypt, was like manna compared with Mrs. Patel's curry.

I looked at my sister, who hadn't shed a tear, and I wondered how it was possible that we should both have been raised on Tilly's bland diet of overcooked meat and vegetables. Evie had changed both inside and out, and I wasn't sure if it was for better or for worse. Even her voice had become louder and more strident, as though she were emulating her African friends. When she had been in Port Elizabeth on her last vacation, she had sat cross-legged on her bed for hours at a time studying Sotho, pronouncing the words over and over again, but when she had tried to communicate with Lena and Beauty in that language, they had understood little because the language of the Transvaal was different from that of the Eastern Cape. However, they were delighted that Evie was taking the trouble to learn an African language and rewarded her with breakfast in bed every day.

"Don't worry, little sister," Evie said. "The meat is made without curry for those who can't handle the heat!"

"Funny," I said. "When can we eat? I'm about to expire."

"You and Mrs. Patel can have dinner now if you like. Sara and I will wait till later."

Mrs. Patel dished up for us both and she sat opposite me at the kitchen table immersed in her plate of food. Whenever I looked up, I caught sight of the red dot on her forehead and the jewel at the side of her nose. I wondered what Uncle Cy would say if he could see me now.

Port Elizabeth and the safe boundaries of my world had receded into a haze. I had promised to telephone my parents, but I would do that later. I was weary; it had been a long day and it wasn't over yet.

13

Whenever my parents entertained in the evenings, they left the front lights on to welcome the guests, so at 8:30 P.M. I did the same thing in Evie's house. Besides, it was creepy walking around in the dim light from two feeble lamps.

"What do you think you're doing?" Evie asked.

"Shedding a little light on the matter. You're having guests, aren't you?"

"D'you want the whole police force converging on this place?" Evie asked. "They don't like multiracial gatherings. You don't know what they'll accuse us of."

"What could they accuse you of?"

"The Immorality Act for one. They've used that before."

I was aghast. "Was it true? Were you doing *it* with a nonwhite?"

"Don't be ridiculous! I don't do *it* with anyone, whether they're pink, white, green, or purple. But they concoct any rubbish just to harass us."

By 9:15, I was reading in bed and dozing, and I wondered if Evie's meeting had been postponed until another evening. I had heard no one enter the house. But then there were voices coming from a back room and the clink of knives and forks.

I put on my dressing gown and crept down the passage. The door was slightly ajar and I could hear Willem's voice. "Evie will distribute the pamphlets that she's duplicated. It's important that you hand them out at the bus stops in the townships when the workers get off the buses tomorrow evening. We must urge them to boycott their jobs on Thursday and Friday. We will not only be striking a blow at the white supremacists, but also presenting ourselves as a unified force."

There was a rumble of agreement from the few people gathered in the room.

"Furthermore," Willem continued, "on Saturday, Sampson and I have something big planned, something that does not involve the rest of you. I would suggest that each of you plan an alibi for that day. The scheme we are involved in has been organized at a much higher level of the organization, and there is some risk involved. Sampson and I will also have an alibi, but I want you to know that if I am caught, I will have nothing to tell the police because I honestly don't know where my orders are coming from. I value my life above all things, and if any damage is done to me, you must believe it is the work of the police."

A black man, whom I presumed to be Sampson, stood up. "I too will not hang myself in a jail cell, nor will I jump out of any interrogation room window. They will have to push me," he said.

Everyone was silent for a moment, thinking private thoughts.

"I'll make coffee now," Evie said. She swung the door wide, startling me. "What the hell are you doing here?"

"I came to meet your friends." She couldn't see my crimson face in the dark passage.

"Come inside then. Everyone, this is my sister Liz. This is Sampson and Irene Sobetwa and Joshua and Miriam Makala, and you've already met Chandra."

I had never been introduced to black people by their first and surnames. The only black people I'd met were servants, and it never occurred to me that they even had surnames.

The company was polite but obviously preoccupied. I slipped out, remembering that I still hadn't phoned my parents. I dialed the operator and heard a click, then my mother was on the line.

"Darling, where have you been? We called you earlier, but we thought you'd be asleep by now. How was your trip? We miss you already." She rambled on and finally my father came to the phone.

"How are you, darling? How is Evie? Can I talk to her?"

"Evie's fine," I said. "We cooked dinner and now there's a meeting going on."

The telephone clicked. "Dad, are you still there?"

"Yes, baby, we'll talk again. Go to bed now."

Evie came out of the kitchen with a coffee tray and a packet of rusks. "What are you doing?" she asked.

"I just called the folks. They send love and Dad wanted to talk to you, but I said you were busy with a meeting."

"You did what?" She flung open the door of the back room. "Leave, everyone! Now! Go right now!"

No one asked any questions, but they left as silently as they had arrived. Only Willem sat drinking coffee at the kitchen table with Sara.

Evie unlocked the wardrobe in her room, took out a pile of pamphlets, dumped them at the bottom of my suitcase, and covered them with clothes.

Someone was knocking viciously on the front door.

"Let those bastards sweat," Evie said.

Finally she opened the door when I thought they would tear it down. Three plainclothes policemen pushed her aside and strode from room to room. When they reached her bedroom, they threw everything out of her trunk and kicked at the door of her wardrobe till it splintered and burst open. They found the duplicating machine and smashed it against the wall. Then they tore out the drawers but found nothing there.

"You got it coming to you, you kaffir-loving bitch," one man said, and I recognized his pock-marked face and greasy, blond hair from the university meeting earlier that day.

"You too, you *wit-kaffir*," he said to Willem, smashing his fist on the kitchen table so that the saucers jumped. Willem continued drinking his coffee, his face a mask, but Sara's eyes were large with terror and I realized that my eyes, too, were twice their normal size.

When they left, Evie had tears in her eyes, though she had shown no fear in their presence. Willem stood up and held her against him until she relaxed. "Please be careful on Saturday," she whispered. "If anything happened to you I couldn't bear it." She wiped her eyes with the back of her hand and then smiled at me reassuringly. "It's OK, kid. Just watch what you say on the phone next time."

14

At Willem's suggestion, Evie agreed to come to Vereeniging with me on Saturday, and my parents were delighted at her apparently renewed interest in the family. Sara, too, decided to take a trip out of town to visit her relatives in Vanderbijlpark, which was a short drive from Vereeniging across the Vaal River. She and Mrs. Patel offered to drop us off on the way to save the Levins a trip into the city.

The small Austin chugged along at a slow pace, weighted down by the luggage and by Mrs. Patel, who sat as large and silent as a sphinx filling the back seat. It was still early morning and the streets were relatively quiet. Outside the city we stopped for petrol.

"I need to go to the toilet," I said.

"So go and hurry up," Evie said. She had been in a bad mood all morning, obviously worried about Willem. They had spoken in whispers for hours the night before, and when Evie had finally come to bed I had listened to her tossing and turning for what seemed like an eternity.

"There's no need to rush, Elizabeth. I need to go, too," Sara said.

"Ugh, it's pretty disgusting. I hate public toilets," I said, coming out of the tiny cubicle at the side of the service station.

Sara emerged a few minutes later holding out her wet hands. "There's nothing to even dry one's hands with."

I was offering her the hem of my skirt when an obese, florid-faced man emerged from the front of the petrol station.

"Hey you, coolie girl, can't you read what the sign says?" His eyes bulged with rage as he raised his arm to a faded EUROPEANS ONLY sign above the toilet door. I thought he would smash his fist down on Sara's head and crack open her skull. She must have had a similar vision, for she cowered and fled to the car. Sara hugged the steering wheel to gain control of herself. She was shaking so much that she could barely start the car.

"You fat pig," I screamed at the man from the safety of the back seat as we finally pulled onto the road.

"Don't waste your breath," Evie said. "He's beyond help."

It was a gray day and the dry grass matched the sky. We drove in silence past fields of bearded mealies and pastures of thickly coated curly-haired sheep. Sara took a detour to the Levins' farmhouse along gravel roads that cut through private farms separated from one another by barbed wire fences and wide gates. Emerging from nowhere, little black urchins ran out to open the gates for us, swinging on the iron bars with hands outstretched for a few pennies.

Aunt Rhoda answered the door as soon as I rang and she hugged me with delight. "I'll send the boy out for the luggage," she said, squinting out at the parked car. "And tell Evie to bring her friends in for something to drink. They must be tired. It's no joke traveling on the bumpy country roads in a car that size."

I ran to the car and invited Sara and her aunt to come inside.

"Come on, you look like an exhausted wreck," Evie cajoled. And after a little further nagging, Sara agreed.

Evie introduced her friends to Aunt Rhoda, who tried to smother her surprise. "Why not go in the kitchen and I'll tell Eunice to give you some tea."

I had never known my aunt or my cousin Lucy to entertain their friends in the kitchen, but I was at least thankful that she didn't tell Sara and Mrs. Patel to use the back door.

Evie watched Eunice take down two enamel mugs and two china cups and saucers for tea and she immediately got up and took down two more china cups and saucers. "You can put these away, Eunice," she said, picking up the mugs.

We didn't see my aunt again until our guests had left, and she wasn't quite as friendly as she had been. "Evelyn, you mustn't interfere with the servants. Eunice is quite upset."

"Eunice is either brainwashed or brainless," Evie said, and I sighed at the thought of what was yet to come, particularly when Evie remet our cousin Lucy, who she said had popcorn between her ears.

Lucy had spent the summer with us when Evie was home from university. While Evie studied the Sotho language at the top of her lungs, Cousin Lucy, only two years my senior, quietly practiced the language of love. And while Evie argued with my father about government policy, Lucy taught me her policies on how to catch the opposite sex. Admirers called constantly begging her for dates, which proved to me that her methods were tried and true.

"I wish Evie would take some tips from her cousin Lucy," my mother had said with a sigh. "That girl has what it takes." I guess I understood what she meant. Lucy was blonde and dimpled and had an enviable chest, and her allure had not escaped a single member of the male population of the summer crowd who flocked to Humewood Beach in search of suntans and female flesh. Nor had her appeal escaped our Aunt Phoebe, who was wont to mumble, "That girl never misses an opportunity to slap her gender in everyone's face."

Lucy had not changed at all since the summer. She bounded into the house in time for lunch, her gender charmingly accentuated by a short tennis skirt. She hugged Evie and me and introduced us to her latest beau, Joey Bloch, who stood in the hallway perspiring from his tennis game. His horn-rimmed spectacles were all steamed up, either from exertion or, possibly, I thought, from the proximity to bare-legged Lucy.

"Well, fair maidens, I shall see you anon," Joey said, finally taking his leave.

"Joey played Hamlet in the school play," Lucy giggled, by way of explaining his dramatic speech. "When the English teacher, Mr. Tubbs, whom we call Tubby 'cos he's so fat, asked Joey to recite Hamlet's soliloquy to the class, Joey stood up, and with a very serious expression on his face, he recited, 'Tubby or not tubby, That is the question.' " She giggled again. "He's really a scream."

Joey was rather plain and thick set, not at all typical of Lucy's boyfriends, but he had apparently won her through persistence and a rare comic ability. But I wondered how long the attraction would last. No one had ever held her interest for more than two weeks at a stretch, although she declared that she and Joey had been going steady for a month.

"Lucy's going to a dance tonight. Can't we arrange a date for you with one of her friends?" Aunt Rhoda asked Evie.

"No thanks," Evie replied with an amused smile. "I'm not in the habit of cradle-snatching. I'm going to walk to the stables and maybe take a ride around the farm."

"Oh well!" Aunt Rhoda sighed, and I knew she was thinking she could tell my mother she had at least tried.

Evie went off to the stables and I stayed with Lucy. We were in the bathroom admiring the grit she had washed out of her hair from the sandy tennis court when the phone rang.

"The phone's ringing," I said.

"Hm, answer it," she said, swishing the basin clean.

"You know it's for you," I said.

"My hair's wet, and anyway, it's not my policy." I knew her policy perfectly well: Keep 'em waiting and don't let them think you're hanging around waiting for calls.

When I heard Joey's distinctive voice on the phone, I said, "I'll call her."

"No, no," he said. " 'Tis your ladyship with whom I wish to converse. What dost thou this eve?"

"Why?" I answered suspiciously, knowing that Joey was taking Lucy to the dance at the country club.

"Well, I have this handsome, brilliant cousin who has just arrived and needs a date. He's going to medical school next year and he's a grandiose tennis player." Joey had adopted his best salesman-of-the-year voice.

"Thanks anyway, but I'm busy tonight." I blushed at the lie and wondered if Joey could detect it. "Tell you what," I added brightly, "I'll ask Lucy to call around and ask if any of her friends are available."

I replaced the receiver, disappointed at the missed opportunity, but I knew Lucy would approve of the way I had handled the situation. "Never accept a last-minute date," she always said. "It's bad policy."

"Who was it?" Lucy asked with concentrated indifference. She had a towel twirled round her wet locks and was studying herself in the long mirror in the bedroom we shared. She would probably spend the rest of the afternoon dabbing stuff on her face and trying out new hairstyles.

"Just Joey trying to fix me up with his gorgeous cousin."

"Good, you'll join us then." She sounded as though she knew all about it.

"No, I told him that I was busy and that you'd call around to see if anyone else was available."

"Are you crazy?" Lucy exploded. "Keep him for yourself."

"I thought you always said I was too young for your crowd," I reminded her.

"So you are. But I told Joey that you were fifteen because I knew his cousin might arrive."

"Well, it's too late now," I said, surprised at her vehemence.

"No it's not. I'll phone Joey myself and tell him you can come."

Lucy's decision was final. She returned from the telephone triumphantly. "It's all arranged. Now sit down and let's see what we can do to make you look a little older."

Changing a snub-nosed, freckle-faced teenager into a sophisticate was a formidable task, and the transformation never quite succeeded. Somehow my freckles would work their way through the camouflage of powder, their presence even more pronounced against the artificially pale background, and my eyes took on a rosy hue as we discovered that I had an allergy to the bright blue eyeliner. But Lucy never gave up. She teased my mousy brown hair into a bird's nest that seemed to grow from my forehead, cheeks, and chin.

"Go wash that muck off your face," Evie said, when she returned later. I noticed that she said nothing to Lucy, who had so subtly enhanced her features that her make-up was barely visible.

"Well, well, quite a beauty treatment," my aunt exclaimed, her voice pitched a little higher than usual. "What are you going to wear, Elizabeth?" I wished I could wear jeans or shorts. I still hated the expensive creations passed down from my cousin Ruthie, who was six feet tall and had constructed an hourglass figure for herself by means of a waist cinch and padded bras. Wearing Ruthie's dresses was always a reminder of the dreaded trips to the cat-filled house of Mrs. Summers, the dressmaker, where I would sneeze and weep allergically as she tucked in the bodice here, let out the waist there, or lopped off a gallon of hem, later to be made into a headband. I must have had a never-to-be-worn sash or headband for every one of Ruthie's dresses.

"Secondhand Rose." I grimaced, as I enviously watched Lucy lay out her new dress at the end of her bed.

"I think the white one with the silver beads round the waist would look great on you," Lucy suggested.

I tried it on, and every other dress that I'd brought, eventually returning to the white one, which made me look like a zeppelin with silver hieroglyphics round the middle. The bodice sagged, so I stuffed my bra with cotton socks. If my mother hadn't spent a fortune on Evie's clothes, which were now distributed throughout the Johannesburg township, perhaps I would have some decent dresses, I thought bitterly. And so much for her grooming money, which was spent on duplicating machines and the like.

"You look sensational," Lucy commented, as she lifted my ridiculous beehive hairdo with the handle of her comb. I couldn't return the compliment because she hadn't slipped into her dress yet. She never did, until the doorbell rang. "Always keep them waiting," she'd say with a half smile, her lashes lowered as though she were hiding a big secret. "It's good policy."

On Lucy's instructions, I answered the door after the second ring. Joey stood there very dapper in his navy suit and horn-rimmed spectacles. "Well, fair maiden," he said, in what my aunt called his gift-of-the-gab voice, "meet my cousin Hotspur, better known as Lester Schwartz."

My eyes traveled up Lester's tall, broad, cream-clad presence, and my expression must have said Wow! because he smiled, revealing flashing white teeth against his perennial tan. The scent of Brilliantine from his pitch-black, slicked-back hair mingled with Old Spice after-shave, and his nostrils flared as he spoke. We went into the lounge, where my uncle and Evie were reading and my aunt was pretending to read. By the time Lucy entered the room, my aunt knew practically all Lester's life story, what his father did for a living, and what his mother's maiden name was. My back was to the door, but I knew when Lucy arrived because Lester started to say something, but no sound emerged. His long, narrow eyes were no longer on my aunt, but had slid sideways to take in a stunning vision in green chiffon. I heard a sigh from Joey and wondered if it was one of admiration or resignation.

"You must be Lester," Lucy said breathily, not removing her large eyes from his face. Then she turned to Joey.

"Sorry if I'm a little late, but I was so engrossed in this medical article I was reading." I looked at Evie and rolled my eyes. Lucy had obviously been preparing to meet Lester, the medical student. The only time she read anything other than *True Romances* was before a date when she wanted to impress. "Doing your homework before a date is good policy," she'd say. But she needn't have bothered this time—Lester was already too distracted for intelligent conversation. In my mind's eye, I could see Lucy and Lester floating through the evening, oblivious even to Joey's halfhearted clowning. He would hold her delicately on the dance floor, like he might a cream bun, not wanting any of the delicious center to escape, while Joey wept on my shoulder, deciding whether to be or not to be!

"Let me know all the details," my aunt insisted as we were leaving. "You'll have to tell us what everyone was wearing and what you had for dinner." Dinner! I was so excited that the thought of food made me ill.

"Have a good time," Evie said quietly to me, pushing a stray hair behind my ear. "Joey will be good company." Her mouth smiled, but her eyes looked so sad that I wondered if she missed the flossy kind of life she'd once had— the parties and dating people like the handsome, suave Lester—or was she just anxious about Willem and his mystery mission?

"I'll see you later. And I'll tell you all about it," I whispered to her with tongue in cheek, letting her know that I knew what to expect.

I never did tell Evie about that evening. She wasn't at the house when we returned. The lights were on in every room, which was quite unlike my aunt Rhoda, who believed in conserving electricity and anything else that cost money, except where her only child was concerned.

My aunt was walking around in her dressing gown, quite hysterical. The Special Branch had come for Evie—God knows why—she'd been at the house all day. And what would the neighbors think, and their friends, if Evie were put in jail? After all, it wasn't like we were distant relatives. And the stigma for her poor parents! On and on she rambled. She had telephoned my father with the news and he was flying to Johannesburg the next day.

The following morning, the Sunday *Times* headlines read JOHANNESBURG–PRETORIA RAILWAY LINES SABOTAGED. In the body of the article was a list of suspects taken into custody. Among the accused held in solitary confinement were the names Willem Coetzee and Sampson Sobetwa. And among those placed under house arrest was Evelyn Ann Levin.

15

Evie was back in Port Elizabeth when I returned. My mother told me that my father had persuaded the Special Branch, in his fluent Afrikaans, to please let Evie remain at home with him where he could keep an eye on her. And he had also explained to them that her interest in politics stemmed from her unhappy past, as she had lost her mother at a tender age. The head of the Special Branch had been quite sympathetic, my mother said, and had offered to lift the ban altogether if Evie would act as an informer for them. My mother, who never swore, would not repeat what Evie had replied to Colonel Prinsloo, but it was something most unladylike. Prinsloo had given my father his private number in case Evie changed her mind at any time. After all, he knew that for a young girl to be confined to her home and to be allowed only one visitor at a time—that is, if anyone would want to visit a political prisoner—was not very pleasant.

"Evie may have had good intentions," my mother said bitterly, "but she's destroyed this family." And I understood that the stigma would always remain and that my father would no longer be quite such "a somebody" in the community.

The fabric of life had changed in other ways in the three weeks I had been gone. Beauty was no longer in the kitchen. She was pregnant by a mysterious stranger whose name she would divulge to no one, although my mother thought she had finally told Lena after Lena had beaten her mercilessly about the face. "You should have heard the caterwauling in the backyard," my mother said. "Like animals. It was a disgrace! I threatened to call the police but Lena knew I wouldn't because Beauty still doesn't have a pass."

Beauty had returned to the Transkei to marry a man who needed a fertile wife. She had been replaced by Florence, an excellent cook, who unfortunately, my mother soon discovered, ran a shebeen in our backyard, supplying her special brew to the *tsotsis* from the golf course. As soon as she could be replaced, Florence would also have to go.

Evie grew thin and pale as she languished in her room from day to day, her only outing a weekly obligatory trip to report to the local police station, and we were constantly aware that our house was under surveillance from a car parked across the street close to the fence of the golf course. Delia and I devised a special code for the telephone, which was undoubtedly bugged, an idea she found thrilling. But Delia didn't have to deal with the day-to-day reality of arriving home from school to the sight of that old Pontiac with its tinted windows that represented our lack of freedom. It was the first sight that greeted me as I turned into Westview Drive when I walked home from the bus stop each day, and today was no different.

I threw down my school case and perched on the window ledge in the porch, still dressed in my navy school uniform, a book lying idly on my lap. Lena was sitting in a wicker chair darning socks. Outside the sky hung like a yellow-gray prairie, washing the flowers and shrubs in an eerie light and illuminating their colors against the dark backdrop of pine trees that edged the golf course. I could smell the sweet, cloying yesterday-today-and-tomorrow shrub with its confetti of tiny flowers, some violet, some purple, and others pure white, and I wondered, as I often had before, which color was meant to represent which moment in time.

"You dreaming again, Miss Liz, 'stead of doing your homework," Lena reprimanded. As I turned to look at her, I caught the smell of freshly ironed laundry airing on the clotheshorse. Tuesday afternoon was her time for mending, and on the table lay an old school case containing threads, needles, and pins. She had thrust a light bulb into the toe of a sock to expose a hole that her nimble fingers were covering with tiny, invisible stitches. I noticed that she had begun to attach "Miss" to my name, as though I were one step away from being "madam."

For a while I went back to my book until the quiet was broken by the rumble of a Pickford's removal truck that stopped next door, outside the Johnsons' house. When I'd first heard the Johnsons were moving away, I had felt uneasy, a temporary remorse that something else was about to change. Only one family had moved from our block since I was born, and I knew every house, both inside and out, and the idiosyncrasies of the people who lived in them. But if I had been told that one family out of the six on our block had to leave and the choice was mine, I probably would have chosen the Johnsons. Brian Johnson still ignored me, and his grown-up sister Elise, with her blonde, wavy hair and flat face, would practice her operatics whenever I tried to study. The high notes would pierce through the hedge of hibiscus, and I would watch the windowpanes to see if they would shatter. The only respite from Elise's singing was when she accidentally swallowed a needle while altering the hem on her white dress for her debut in Handel's *The Messiah*. I imagined she must have held the needle between her lips, and then in a forgetful moment probably broke into song. I never could put a needle or pin near my lips without my mother reminding me about the cotton-wool sandwich that the doctor had made Elise swallow.

No one was there to wish the Johnsons a final farewell. The street was deserted except for the Pickford's men loading furniture, heavy stinkwood tables and chairs, and velvet-upholstered sofas haphazardly draped with protective sheets. The men were tall and strong with sullen faces, and they were not too gentle with the furniture. Mr. Johnson followed them in and out of the house gesticulating anxiously, but the men ignored him. One bent to pick a long stem of grass, which he chewed and then left hanging from the side of his mouth.

"The street is so empty, no one wants to be caught in the storm," I said to Lena, who had stood up to stretch her legs.

She jabbed me and nodded toward the trees. "Some people not worried about the weather, Miss Liz."

Only then did I notice three *tsotsis* almost blending into the dark pines. How long had they been there? One sucked on a cigarette "stompie," and another whipped a nettle against the fence in a slow, rhythmic motion. I hadn't seen them before.

"The Johnsons better take everything they got or those *skollies* going to take it for sure," Lena said.

I could picture a swarm of *skollies* darting like lizards across the road to the Johnsons' house, easing their slender, unwashed bodies through the narrow windows and burglar bars, taking a warm blanket or some clothing to their tin shanty on the golf course. Worse still, I imagined them living in the house secretly until the new neighbors arrived.

A gust of wind came up and Mr. Johnson looked forlorn, his too-wide trousers flapping against his skinny legs.

"I wonder why Mrs. Johnson isn't running the show," I said.

"She probably in the hospital with Miss Elise. Beside, she never want to see this house again."

"Did Elise swallow another needle?" I snickered, knowing full well I was not to ask the servants about this. My mother had said that all I needed to know was that because of Elise's illness, the Johnsons were moving to a flat on a brightly lit street always streaming with noisy traffic. I had begged to hear what else the grown-ups were whispering about behind closed doors. But now, as Lena suddenly said, "You big gel now, you should know." I wanted to withdraw to safety, to put my hands over my ears and remind her of my mother's wishes.

"Miss Elise been attacked," Lena said.

Attacked! It was such a strange word. The only attack I'd witnessed had been in the game reserve, where we'd watched a lion kill a buck just a few feet from our car. Everyone had said how lucky we were to witness the attack and kill, but I had felt sick to my stomach at the sight of gushing blood and the terror in the eyes of the buck. But I knew Elise's attack must have been different.

"You mean the *tsotsis* got her, don't you?"

130

"One evening Miss Elise she alone at the house. A man, a man in a clean suit, he knock at the door and he say, 'Please madam, I want something to eat, just a loaf of bread, I am out of a job.' She close the door, but she not lock it while she go to the kitchen for bread. When she come back, the man is inside the door."

So it wasn't even a *tsotsi,* I thought. A wolf in sheep's clothing came to mind—my mother was always saying those kinds of things. "Wasn't Lettie there?" I asked.

"She was in her room in the yard. But Lettie is a new gel. You know *that* madam, she cannot keep a gel for very long."

"But didn't Lettie hear her . . . hear anything?" I asked.

Lena shrugged. "Mebbe. Mebbe not." She seemed unconcerned. And then I thought of Brian and of Beauty pregnant. And through my mind flashed a phrase: An eye for an eye. . . .

The wind was getting stronger now and I could see blood-red petals falling from the poinsettia bush beneath the window. They blew around on the grass. I closed the window and hugged my knees to my chest. I noticed that the *tsotsi* boys had vanished from the golf course.

"Maybe I heard her scream," I whispered. "Maybe I thought it was just another high note."

"Un-un-un." Lena shook her head. "That poor gel, she not going to be singing around here any more." Her face was impassive.

16

Not only were our household and neighborhood in transition, but the school atmosphere had subtly changed as well. Delia was more distant since she had acquired a steady boyfriend who she admitted had *vreyed* her. At the look of shock on my face, she immediately said that she was just teasing, that she would never let anyone touch her boobs. But I knew she had, and to me she began to look more and more like the girl on the train to whom Barry Kaliff had given his Star of David.

Since Evie had made headlines in the local newspaper, the other girls at school had stood around in groups, tittering behind my back. But all the snickering stopped when Irmgard Dietrich stuck her forefinger into my nipple, twisting her hand around like a dagger. "You commie Jew!" she spat out. I knew she spoke for the rest of the students at Queen Victoria High School who held me responsible for my sister's convictions—the kind of convictions that could unsettle their charmed lives.

The assault took place under the gnarled, old oak tree in the playground as we waited to march back to class after a game of volleyball. Thoughts of permanent deformity flashed through my mind as I instinctively hit Irmgard's offending arm, causing her hand to shoot upward and dislodge her glasses, which smashed on the asphalt. Her thick, protruding lower lip quivered for an instant before she yelled to the teacher on duty. "Miss Cox!"

It must have been the note of hysteria that brought Miss Cox running. Miss Cox never ran, and under normal circumstances she would have given the insolent girl fifty lines to write—something ridiculous like, *I must not shout out a teacher's name in vain*—to cure her of her rudeness. Miss Cox's stern eyes took in the smashed lenses and Irmgard's accusing finger pointed at me.

"Elizabeth," she said, "go immediately to the principal's office."

That very morning in history class, after we had read about Germany's part in the Second World War, Miss Cox had looked at us with her owl eyes and said, "One outstanding trait of the Jews that we can all learn from is that they never fight back. History has shown them to be a passive and forgiving people." I had proved her wrong, and she took my retaliation as a personal affront.

Instead of going to the principal's office, I went to my classroom and packed my case, then walked out of the school's gates with the intention of never returning. I expected voices to call me back, to reprimand me for leaving without permission, but no one even noticed.

I also had no intention of returning home to the sinister parked car with its anonymous driver and to Evie listlessly knitting while my mother chirped away in an effort to keep up everyone's spirits. Secretly she told me that this whole business was killing my father, and it would be best for everyone if Evie could leave the country and start a new life for herself away from the influence of that Coetzee boy. My mother's younger brother and his family, who lived in England, were also bleeding-heart liberals and would be happy to have Evie stay with them. But she would have to wait till her banning order was over, and then there was no guarantee that they wouldn't renew it. Also, it was highly unlikely that the government would ever give her a passport. Whenever my mother was in one of her confiding moods, she would turn up the radio and speak in a whisper, in case the walls had ears.

I walked past the school bus stop, crossed Western Road, and hesitated at the edge of the Donkin Reserve, a deserted common that curved like a parabola to the edge of town, serving as a shortcut and a favorite haunt for hobos and drunks who hung around the bar of the nearby Palmerston Hotel.

Queen Vic girls were forbidden to walk on the Donkin alone, and my heart pounded as I heard footsteps behind me. Glancing back, I saw a Colored man running toward me. I panicked and ran, too, wondering if I should throw down my suitcase, which was hindering my speed. I thought of Elise, who had been attacked in her home, which somehow seemed preferable to being found ravaged in a public place.

"Miss Liz, Miss Liz!" I turned to look back, and now I recognized Popeye. He was out of breath, running with a limp, and in his hand was a bottle that he held out in front of him as though offering me a drink. He no longer worked for my father on a regular basis, but came and went as he pleased, preferring that my father pay him by the hour.

Popeye sat down on a wooden bench, out of breath. "I heard from my boy, you know. He managed to get out a

134

note to his mother, and this one's for your sister." He took a dirty, crumpled envelope from his pocket. It wasn't sealed. "I put it in the envelope," he said. "You can read it."

The scruffy note with its torn edges was written in pencil and could fit in the palm of my hand.

"But this was written a month ago," I said.

Popeye shrugged. "It came about three weeks ago. I was going to bring it to the house, but that blerry car's outside all the time and I didn't want to give it to your pa. You read what he says. Those bastards must be making him pay. You can be sure they're torturing him good and proper." Popeye raised his hand to his face and stuck his thumb and forefinger into his closed eyelids. I thought he was going to cry, but then I could hear him praying.

"I have to go now," I said, seeing someone in a navy uniform approaching. Soon, groups of Queen Vic girls would be walking into town and I wanted to avoid them. Popeye didn't hear me. He was in another world, mumbling to his God in a drunken incantation.

"That Colored bothering you?" Sybil Carter came up to me.

"No, he just works for my dad."

"You walking into town? Want to come to the Willowtree?"

Sybil Carter had the worst reputation at Queen Vic, and I knew that the Willowtree was where she hung out in the afternoons with her boyfriend, Duke, and his gang—the gang of which Barry Kaliff had been a proud member.

"Sure, why not!" I already had a reputation for being a commie; I might just as well have one for being a "sheila."

First we went to the rest room in Garlicks department store, where Sybil shoved her school hat into her satchel, which contained no books. She never did homework. She teased her hair around her face, applied lipstick and false eyelashes, raised the collar of her blazer, and pushed the sleeves up to three-quarter length. Finally, she puckered up her uniform at the waist so that the hem displayed more leg.

We strolled into the Willowtree, where a greasy-haired, leather-jacketed group played pinball and fed coins into a jukebox. Elvis's voice vibrated through the room. Duke dislodged himself from the rest and, without a word, walked up to Sybil, put his hand on her behind, and crushed her to him. He kissed her on the mouth, then walked away, ignoring her for a while. Then he came back. "Who's this?" he asked, looking at me.

"Jus' a school friend. Name's Elizabeth," Sybil said, pouting.

"She stuck up or something?"

"Ag, Duke, jus' leave her alone, man!"

Sybil and I shared our problems over a float. Her life was simple compared with mine. Maybe God was punishing me, I told her. It had occurred to me many times that none of this would have happened if I hadn't introduced Willem to Evie at the station.

"Ag, that's not true," Sybil said. "If it wasn't this Willem guy, it would have been someone else. It's like me and Duke. If I wasn't doing it with him, I'd be doing it with someone else."

I was so startled by her admission that it took me a while to figure out her logic. I'd always wondered whether she'd really done it, or whether it was just talk. Somehow it seemed all right for girls like her, and at the same time I realized that I wasn't going to make the grade as a sheila.

A small, blue Anglia was parked outside our house when I finally got home, and I recognized it as belonging to the nuns. Since my mother's hysterectomy, the nuns had visited at least once a month, and since Evie's house arrest they had come more often, to give moral support, my mother said.

Chopin was playing loudly on the record player, which meant that my mother must be discussing something private. The nuns sat like three ravens, their heads perked forward, listening to my mother. When she saw me she roared, "Where have you been? I've been so worried. I called Delia and she said you may have had detention, and I called the school but no one had seen you. Don't I have enough troubles already?"

"I was in town," I said quietly.

"Next time you phone me, do you hear?"

The nuns surveyed me. "Listen to your mother and you'll never go wrong," Sister Katherine intoned.

I left them to their private discussion and went to Evie's room. She was asleep, so I sat in the porch and contemplated Willem's note over a glass of milk and Marie biscuits. I could be sitting in the very chair that Willem had sat in more than a year ago when he had watched me play tennis against the wall, I thought.

"What's that, Liza?" My mother's voice startled me. I hadn't noticed the nuns leaving the house, and now my mother was nodding at the note in my hand.

"I bumped into Popeye and he gave me this note from Willem to give to Evie."

My mother read the note softly.

"Darling, this is going to upset your sister terribly. Wait until after Ruthie's wedding on Sunday before you give it to her. She's been so looking forward to her first social event for so long, and you know what trouble Daddy went to to get permission for her to attend the wedding."

My mother's request sounded quite reasonable. I would give Evie the note after the wedding, which was only three days away. Meantime I would keep it safely hidden between the pages of my diary in my bedside drawer.

17

Aunt Phoebe wanted her daughter's wedding to be like no other celebration. Nothing was left to chance, for she didn't want to give the gossips an opportunity to make a single disparaging remark about *the* coming event of the year, as she so boldly named it. My mother crossed her fingers and said, "Please God," every time Aunt Phoebe spoke about the wedding because she still didn't believe one should cross one's bridges . . . or count one's chickens.

Ruth had wanted Evie to be her maid of honor, but whether Evie could even attend the wedding was too uncertain at that time. Thus Lucy, the next eldest cousin, was selected, and I was to be one of the bridesmaids.

Several months before the event, Aunt Phoebe had arrived with a swatch of pale yellow *broderie anglaise* material and a bridesmaid's pattern. I looked at my mother and she knew my thoughts immediately—yellow was not my color. I would look thoroughly insipid, and in fact, so would everyone else in the retinue.

"Ruthie chose the bridesmaid's material and pattern herself," Aunt Phoebe boasted.

"I'm sure she did," I said.

Aunt Phoebe looked at me sharply, but I just smiled sunnily, to my mother's relief. I wasn't going to tell my aunt that her beloved Ruthie was making sure that none of the members of her retinue would outshine her at the altar on her momentous day.

"Now I'm going to tell you a secret," my aunt had whispered through the side of her mouth as if she were about to divulge a juicy piece of gossip. "Her name is Winnie."

"Who is Winnie?" my mother asked, bewildered.

"The dressmaker, of course. The best."

"What about Mrs. Summers?" I asked.

"Oh, she's fine for alterations, but Winnie is an artist—and don't you go telling a living soul about her."

"She must charge a fortune," my mother said dubiously.

"No, she's even cheaper than Mrs. S. She's a Colored woman," my aunt explained.

When Aunt Phoebe had driven away, I asked my mother why she had never mentioned Winnie before.

"Oh, you know your aunt and her crowd. They don't want anyone to know who sews for them, otherwise their dressmakers might get too busy and too independent."

Winnie came to the house for fittings, and with her expertise, my bridesmaid's dress turned out to be far prettier than I had imagined. My mother had also bought yards of deep blue chiffon for a dress for Evie, in the hope that she would be allowed to attend the wedding.

Evie enjoyed the fittings, which were salted by Winnie's unsubtle brand of humor. "Ag, Miss Eve, you's going to get your Adam one of these days!" Winnie would exclaim. And one afternoon, when Winnie met Jeremy Samuels, who was home for a vacation, she winked conspiratorially and grinned, baring a gummy space where her two front teeth should have been. "Ag, Miss Eve, you catch the bo-ket at the wedding and you sure to be next," Winnie pre-dicted. As the dresses came close to completion, Lena, too, never missed a fitting. She would stand in the doorway, stomping her feet and clapping ecstatically. "My gels going to be the best," she would say. But, when the dresses were finally hanging in the wardrobe, draped in tissue pa-per, the excitement died down until the weekend of the wedding.

Traditionally, the bride and groom were not allowed to see each other on the day of the wedding, so Selwyn spent his last night as a bachelor at our house. Early on Sunday morning, I walked into the porch and found Selwyn sitting there, enunciating over and over again, "H-ow n-ow br-own c-ow."

He looked sheepish when he saw me.

"What on earth are you doing?" I asked in a voice that said, Now I've seen everything!

"Ruthie's been giving me speech lessons so I won't make a fool of myself at the wedding. That was one of her exercises. Can I practice my speech in front of you now?" he asked, nervously clutching a sheet of paper.

"Of course," I said, and then added sweetly, "but if Cousin Ruthie prefers her own accent to yours, perhaps you should have told her to make the speech."

Later on in the day, Evie and I were dressing when Lucy arrived with her parents from the hotel where they were staying. She carried her dress covered in plastic—no doubt she would only slip it on at the last minute. We were ready to leave for the synagogue when Lucy finally appeared. I knew she had entered the room because Selwyn stood riveted with his jaw open in midspeech—a reminder of the late Lester, as Lucy named her ex-beau, Lester Schwartz, since discarding him for someone else.

My father nudged Selwyn out of his daze, and I heard him whisper in an amused tone, "My boy, at this stage you can only look and long."

Lucy had used neither the pattern nor the material given to her by Aunt Phoebe. She wore a deep yellow, tight-fitting, Spanish-style dress with a frill around the shoulders and another around the hem that was long at the back and curved upward in front to display her knees.

"Aunt Phoebe's going to have a cadenza," I said to Lucy.

"Good, I like to give people cadenzas." She giggled.

We all hovered around Lucy at the synagogue, waiting for Aunt Phoebe's reaction, which was surprisingly re-strained. "My girl, I think you forgot your castanets" was all she said, and when I saw Cousin Ruthie looking like a goddess in white lace, I understood Aunt Phoebe's calm, for no one could eclipse the bride on her wedding day.

The ceremony and reception went without a hitch. My parents sat at the main table with the bride and groom and aunts and uncles, while Evie and I sat at the table reserved for the retinue. She invited Jeremy Samuels to sit with her. As the band struck up, Ruthie and Selwyn took the floor for the first waltz, which I was sure she had made him practice ad nauseam. Then Evie and Jeremy floated away, and she seemed to sparkle as she hadn't done in months. It had occurred to me during the evening that no one at our table spoke to Evie, as though they were scared to spark off a conversation that might lead to a political discussion.

At one point, the band took a break and Jeremy, who had been discussing Evie's future with her, turned to me and said, "And you, Liz, what are you planning to do when you leave school?"

The general conversation at the table had waned, and everyone was looking at me expectantly. "I'd like to be a lawyer."

"Uh-huh. Where do you want to study?"

"At Cape Town University." I didn't add that my father had said he would never allow me to go to Wits.

"You know if you study law in South Africa you won't be able to practice anywhere else, because none of the other English-speaking countries uses Roman-Dutch law."

"I wasn't planning to go anywhere else," I said.

"Always keep your options open," Jeremy said.

"Why would you want to do law?" someone asked.

"Maybe I'll be able to do some good—like defending political prisoners."

"I'm afraid you won't get much work in that line," Evie said drily. "In case you haven't noticed, political prisoners rarely get tried."

Someone coughed uncomfortably, and everyone looked relieved as the band began playing again.

Later in the evening, in the midst of the revelry, I noticed Evie staring into space. Her face was white and she shivered as though blasted by an icy wind. "I have to go," she said. "I feel strange."

Jeremy willingly offered to take her home, and I wondered if the earlier conversation had upset her. As they left the hall, a man slipped out after them. I walked to the door and saw Jeremy's car being trailed. Even tonight Evie was being watched.

When I returned home with my parents after midnight, Evie was fast asleep under a pile of blankets, despite the warmth of the night. I was still in my bridesmaid's dress, brushing out my unnaturally teased hair when I heard a low wail, like that of an animal in pain, coming from the backyard. My mother must have heard it, too, for we met at the back door and agreed that the sound was coming from Lena's room. We knocked on the door and pushed it open. On a chair sat Beauty, a thinner version of her formerly plump self, and tied to her back with a blanket was a chubby, sleeping infant. Lena lay on the bed, her eyes like slits in her swollen face.

"They taking my boy," she cried over and over. "Those *tsotsi* soldiers they threatening to kill my boy if he don't come with them. Then they sending him to another country to become fighter. When he come back he will not be knowing his mother. He will be like a dead son to me."

My mother clucked sympathetically and explained that this was something Lena had been afraid of for some time, that young militants were threatening to kill school boys in the homelands if they didn't follow their orders to be trained as guerilla soldiers. The older Africans, like Lena, she said, also wanted change, but not through violent means.

"You must be telling no one," Lena said fearfully. "Otherwise the police they will be after me to find my son."

"We know nothing," my mother said, and I nodded in agreement. Then she looked at Beauty, the bearer of bad tidings. "Why don't you sleep in your old room tonight, Beauty, and let Lena get some rest."

With the excitement of the wedding, and the trauma of Lena's personal drama, Willem's note lay forgotten between the pages of my diary until two days after the wedding. Evie was in the bathroom taking a shower when I found the note.

"It's midafternoon," I shouted next to the curtain. "Why are you showering now?"

"It's all the same to me," Evie replied. "Day is night, night is day." She had been sounding depressed again since the wedding was over.

"Keep the water running. I have something to tell you," I whispered, as she emerged from the shower cubicle.

Evie held up the dirty piece of paper as though it were fragile, then she mouthed the words I had already seen: *Be strong. I can bear the pain knowing we'll be together someday. john.*

"Why does he sign it John, and how do you know it's from him?"

"It's his writing, and John is a private joke. His initials are W. C., which stands for 'water closet,' or the john!"

Evie covered her face with her hands. "Oh God, they must be torturing him. I'm not waiting any longer. I'm going to phone that Colonel Prinsloo and pretend I'll be an informer. Maybe that way I can bargain for Willem."

"You're crazy," I said. "Those Special Branch types aren't stupid."

"I've been thinking about this for a while now," she said, with a determined look on her face.

Evie went to my father's room in her dressing gown, her hair still dripping wet. Colonel Prinsloo's number was under the glass next to the telephone on his bedside table.

"I'm going to listen on the hall phone," I said, but I don't think she even heard. She sat strumming her fingers on the bed, staring at the number. It took a while to get through to Colonel Prinsloo, and then he was on the line. "*Ja,* Prinsloo here."

"Yes, this is Evelyn Levin." Evie's voice shook and then she gained control. "I've been thinking about your offer, and I'm willing to help you in exchange for the release of a friend of mine."

"And who might that be?" Prinsloo sounded quite friendly.

"Willem. Willem Coetzee."

"Ag, but you're a little late, young lady. You see I got word a little while ago about our prisoner Coetzee. Seems he couldn't handle solitary. Some of them can't, especially ones like Coetzee who are used to being on stage all the time."

"What's happened to him?" Evie's voice was low and trembling.

"Like I said, Coetzee couldn't take it. Jumped from the interrogation room window Sunday evening."

There was a pause as the news sank in, and a picture flashed through my mind of Evie pale and shivering at the wedding on Sunday evening.

"Murderer!" Evie screamed. "You bloody murderers, you pushed him!"

I heard the phone crash against the table. When I ran to my parents' room, the mouthpiece dangled an inch from the floor and Evie was crouched on the bed sobbing, her wet hair spreading a dark halo on the white pillowcase.

18

Evie cried for three days following that phone call. In desperation my mother called the family doctor, who gave her a sedative. Dr. Gelbart and my mother spoke in whispers for a long time, and when he finally left, she had a look of determination on her face that I hadn't seen there before.

At Mrs. Coetzee's request, Willem's body was shipped to Port Elizabeth, and several days after the doctor's visit, the funeral was to take place at the South Kloof cemetery. None of our family planned to be there. In accordance with her banning order, Evie was not allowed to attend gatherings of any sort, and my father chose not to go. He decided it would not be a good move politically, and I thought how cautious he had become, and how the spunk had gone out of him since the start of this business with Evie. In the space of months, he had grown stooped and his eyes had lost their mischievous light. He had even bought a new sterilizer for his "white" surgery, but only, he said, because his growing practice required it.

On the day of Willem's funeral, Lena asked for the afternoon off. I watched as she walked through the yard in her black church-choir dress with its white collar and cuffs.

"I didn't know you had church in the middle of the week," I called.

"Not chech," Lena said. "Funeral. Going to funeral for man who die for our cause. The whole of New Brighton going to be there." She made a dramatic arc with her arm.

"It's Willem's funeral. You know Evie's friend—the one who used to come to the house."

"*Hayi kona!*" Lena was shocked.

"I want to come," I said on the spur of the moment, a certainty welling up inside me that I ought to be there.

"You cannot come," Lena said firmly. "Fest of all, you still in school uniform. Second of all, the madam she give me off till Monday night, so I cannot bring you home."

"For heaven's sake, I'm not a baby. I can catch the bus on my own."

"Two buses," she said.

"And my school uniform is perfect for a funeral!" Contrary to my vow never to set foot in Queen Vic ever again, I had returned with my head held high, determined to ignore the groups of whispering girls who had eyed me while talking behind their cupped palms. Surprisingly, no one seemed to snicker anymore. The incident with Irmgard had cleared the air.

"Ma, I'm going to a friend's house," I yelled. "I'll be back later."

"Be careful," she shouted back, but she didn't sound overly concerned. She had been busy these past few days plotting and planning, as she called it, though for what I did not know.

The bus into town was relatively empty, but from the town to South Kloof we were squashed together into a single body, dangerously spilling out onto the platform.

The cemetery stood atop a hill overlooking a disused rail yard on the outer edge of the harbor. The wind blew in from the sea as if to tear the thorn bushes and long, limp strands of grass from their roots in the sandy soil. Grit from the gravel path edged inside my shoes, and Lena had to stop several times to catch her breath. Below us, like swarms of ants, people converged from all directions as though the wind had blown them to the edge of the steep path—black people in dark dresses, Indians in saris, poor Coloreds and well-dressed Coloreds, a few Chinese, and a smattering of white faces.

Among the gray, granite tombstones decorated with benevolent figurines of winged angels and elaborate crosses, the mourners stood still and sullen, and it seemed to me, for an instant, that they were the dead risen from the graves. I could see nothing of the ceremony from where I stood, so I left Lena and wound my way forward in time to see the plain, wooden coffin being lowered into the gaping ground. And then I heard the dull thud of earth as it fell on the coffin. "Dust to dust . . ." the minister intoned, and it didn't seem possible that Willem was in that box—Willem with his animated, intelligent face and his charisma that had kept an entire hall of students spellbound and had swept Evie off her feet the first time she'd met him; Willem who had motivated me to my first major tennis victory. Now he was being mourned by hundreds of people who didn't even know him, but knew what he stood for. His mother stood alone, grasping a balled handkerchief in her tight fist. I couldn't see Popeye but I imagined he was there somewhere.

The minister's speech was over and suddenly the voices of hundreds of mourners rose into the wind. "*Nkosi Sikelel'i Afrika.* . . ." With their right arms raised, they sang the

African national anthem, and their voices were so pure that tears stung my eyes and I could feel goose bumps rising on my arms. I wished that the wind, blowing inland, would carry the sound all the way to our house for Evie to hear.

An Indian couple was standing on either side of Mrs. Coetzee and I ran over to them. "Sara! Chandra!" People were shaking Mrs. Coetzee by the hand, and then it was my turn. She put her hands on my shoulders, drawing me close. My hands hung awkwardly, and I didn't know what to say. "I wish you long life," I said, remembering what people had said to my father when he was sitting *shiva* for my grandfather.

Mrs. Coetzee was unaware of my discomfort. She spoke to me urgently. "Mr. Coetzee left the house when we got the news and he hasn't returned since." She tried to blink back her tears. "Tell your daddy to find him, please my girlie." I wanted to apologize that my father wasn't there, but I kept quiet.

Sara and Chandra had driven down from Johannesburg for the funeral and to see Evie before they left for England. They no longer needed a chaperone. Three months earlier, Evie had received a wedding invitation rudely opened and left unsealed by those anonymous people who opened her letters.

"How was your wedding?" I asked, noting how Sara had filled out and looked more beautiful than ever.

"The wedding was a family affair, which meant that the entire community was there because everyone is directly or indirectly related to everyone else! We brought photographs to show you."

"You here alone?" Chandra asked.

"Uh huh."

"We'll take you home, so you can show us the way."

"Evie's expecting us," Sara said, noticing my hesitation. "I phoned earlier and, of course, I stated quite clearly, for anyone listening, that we would see her one at a time."

"She doesn't look too good," I warned them.

"That's to be expected, but soon everything is going to change. Your mother has been in touch with us."

I wanted to ask what she meant, but Chandra gave her a look and changed the subject.

At the house, Sara brought out her wedding photos, and my mother exclaimed how wonderful that Evie's friends would be in England. I thought how insincere my mother could be at times, since she always said she would hate to leave the South African way of life and return to cold, clammy England.

"I can't wait," Evie said, and her eyes looked brighter than I had seen them in a long time.

"For what?" I asked.

My mother put her fingers to her lips. "It's all arranged," she whispered, while the radio blared. "But!"—she drew a finger across her mouth—"you keep *shtum*, understand!"

The following day was Friday. My mother made breakfast, and my father took Evie to report to the local police station as he did every Friday before he went to work. When he dropped her back at the house, he looked haggard, and hugged her as though he would never see her again. "It's OK, Popsicle," she said, "I'm going to be fine."

At ten o'clock, two of the nuns arrived for morning tea. Sister Katherine carried a large bag. They went into Evie's room, and while the kettle boiled, my mother scraped back Evie's thick hair and pinned it down. Sister Katherine placed the firm, white edge of the black veil against my sister's forehead.

Two nuns and a "novice" had tea on the porch with my mother. Then Evie came into my room, where I lay in bed with stomach cramps. My mother hadn't believed that I felt too ill to go to school. "You just don't want to miss out on anything," she had said. And then when I had winced, she had said it was probably just the excitement.

"So this is it, little sister." Evie took in a deep breath, as though filling her lungs with the sweet air of a home she might never see again. "Just remember to always keep fighting."

"For what?" I asked. "I don't want to end up like you or Willem."

"There are other ways," she said. "You're smarter than I am. You'll find your own way. I know you'll fight for what is right." Her eyes shone and her cheeks were flushed. She made a very pretty nun.

"I'm not even sure what's right."

"Yes you are! Just take a look around you."

I looked around my room, at the wooden furniture and flowered curtains faded from the sunlight. I knew that was not what she meant. But these were the things that she was having to sacrifice, and I didn't ever want to be forced to leave everything that was familiar.

I got out of bed to give her a hug in her strange garb. At the door she turned and looked back at me. "Oh my God," she said. "You finally have your period!"

I looked down at my blood-stained pajama pants. I was almost fifteen years old and still hadn't had "the curse." I had been to the doctor, who pronounced me a late bloomer, but my mother thought I should keep it to myself, just in case. No man would take seriously a wo-man who couldn't bear children. And I had thought of

152

Beauty, whose proven fertility had made her an acceptable wife.

"I'll get Mom," Evie said. I noticed she didn't call her Lydia.

Later, my mother said it was a good omen that I had reached womanhood on the day that Evie left, and I accused her of creating her own superstitions. But she may have been right. On Monday, three tense days after Evie's departure, a telegram arrived from her brother in England: *Thank you for the precious gift. Arrived intact. We will cherish.*

On Tuesday morning, Lena, having returned from her extended weekend off, took breakfast to Evie's room and found it empty. "Madam, madam. Miss Evie gone!"

My mother threw up her hands and gasped. "Don't worry, Lena," she said. "I'll deal with it." She found Colonel Prinsloo's number and dialed carefully. Her voice quavered when she finally got through. "This is Mrs. Levin, Evelyn Levin's mother. I'm afraid I have to report her missing. When the maid took her breakfast this morning, she wasn't there." Then my mother began to sob and I watched with fascination her realistic performance, until I realized she was shedding real tears into her Irish linen handkerchief.

That day, my father returned home from work earlier than usual and I found him sitting lifelessly on the bed in her empty room. He looked around and then he said, "The police found Mr. Coetzee out at Swartkops. His car was in the brush above the sea. He'd used gas. God, how he loved that boy!" He let out a bark that I thought must have been a laugh, but I saw his crumpled face and realized it was a

153

sob. I had never seen my father cry, and I knew his tears weren't just for Popeye.

"This country is a one-way street, and God help you if you ignore the signs and go the wrong way," he said, shaking his head.

"Daddy," I said, no longer able to contain the burden of guilt I'd been harboring since hearing Colonel Prinsloo's terrible pronouncement to Evie on the telephone. "I'm the one who killed Willem, and now Popeye!" My eyes brimmed with tears. "If I'd given Willem's note to Evie on the day I got it, she could have saved his life."

"Ah, my girl!" My father held me close. "You can't blame yourself. Your sister was naïve to think she could make a deal with Prinsloo. You have to understand that those people would never let someone like Willem live. He was a remarkable leader, and nothing terrifies the government more than charismatic leaders with liberal ideals. Popeye knew, and Willem knew too, that it was just a matter of time. The boy was prepared to be a martyr."

I shivered. "I don't ever want to die like that."

"God forbid! But if you don't know it yet, you will eventually realize that you have too much heart to stay here. There is room in this country for only two types of people: Those who believe in the system, and those who passively abide by it."

"But what about those who are willing to fight?" I ventured, thinking of Evie's parting exhortation.

"Haven't you seen enough to know the answer to that question?" My father's voice was bitter. "Dying or being imprisoned for your ideals won't change a thing, and the black man won't even thank you for it. One day, when Lena's son returns like a mindless fighting machine and you are standing in his path, he's not going to know that

154

you are the white girl his mother loves like her own daughter. Nor is he going to stop and think, Ah, let's spare this one, she truly has a good heart."

I closed my eyes against the picture he was creating. "You paint a brutal picture, Daddy."

"A realistic one, my baby, but believe me, I hope I'm wrong."

"Dad?" My chest was constricted with fear. "I don't want to leave yet."

"Of course not, sweetheart, I'm talking about the future. The time will come when you will want to leave, and as much as I dread that day, I won't stop you." He gave a defeated sigh, and the lines of his face were valleys of sadness. "There'll come a time when all our children will want to leave."

I knew, then, that he meant not only his own children, but the country's young people. And I had a vision of parents growing old, alone, and brothers and sisters scattered across the globe, wherever they could find refuge.

I was crying softly now in the dark room. Evie could never again return, and I hoped I would never be in her shoes. "I always want to be able to come back."

"Of course," my father said. "Always."

First Willem, then Jeremy, and now my father! They had all foreseen a future for me someplace else, a future I had refused to contemplate. But perhaps Evie knew me best. She knew that I could not leave without a fight. She had said I would find my own way. Others could wield sticks and stones, but I knew the weapon I would use: Words! I could always fight with words. "Sticks and stones may break my bones, but words will never hurt me," I had long ago shrieked at Fiona Frazer when her words, like arrows, had pierced me to the very core.

As I dried my eyes in the darkening room, my path suddenly seemed perfectly clear, and wherever Evie was at that moment, thousands of miles away, struggling to find refuge, I felt closer to her than I had in a long time.